HARVEST AMERICAN
Writing

MESSENGER
BIRD

Other Books by Dan McCall

Triphammer

The Silence of Bartleby

Queen of Hearts

Bluebird Canyon

Beecher

Jack the Bear

The Man Says Yes

The Example of Richard Wright

Dan McCall

MESSENGER BIRD

A HARVEST BOOK

HARCOURT BRACE & COMPANY

San Diego   New York   London

Library of Congress Cataloging-in-Publication Data
McCall, Dan.
Messenger Bird/Dan McCall. — 1st Harvest ed.
p.   cm. — (A Harvest book) (Harvest American writing series)
ISBN 0-15-600042-3 (pbk.)
1. Indians of North America — New Mexico — Fiction. 2. Apache
Indians — Fiction. 3. New Mexico — Fiction. I. Title. II. Series:
Harvest American writing.
PS3563.C334M46   1994
813'.54 — dc20   94-13239

Designed by Lisa Peters
Printed in the United States of America
First Harvest edition 1994
A B C D E

FOR JANE

M E S C A L E R O , New Mexico, is a beautiful
and heartbreaking real place. *Messenger Bird* is a novel;
the imaginary characters are not
intended to resemble real persons in Mescalero
or anywhere else.

MESSENGER
BIRD

S ▲
U I C I D E   W A S   C O M M O N   among the Apaches of southern New Mexico. One night an important chief about seventy years old was brought up the front steps of the hospital and deposited in the front hallway by a dozen wailing family members and friends. The old man had taken a .22 rifle, put it between his eyes, and pulled the trigger. But he was still alive, and I was expected to keep him that way.

On closer inspection I discovered that the old man had a neat little bullet hole just above his nose and an exit wound forward on his head. He was only semiconscious and was weakly gasping for breath, but it looked like he might be salvageable. In a situation like this, before anything else is done you have to establish a good airway to keep the patient breathing, and at first I thought I should do it the easy way, which is to punch a hole with a knife above that little cartilage like a ring under the Adam's apple. But even though you can do that very quickly, it can damage the vocal cords. I decided to go for a more permanent tracheostomy, which is a little lower. Then, suddenly, the whole hospital went dark. All the lights had gone out, and I was the only one on duty who knew how to start up the generator. I couldn't go down into the basement and do it, though, because this old man was lying on the floor dying. His relatives were moaning and crying out.

So I got to do my first tracheostomy on a green linoleum floor by flashlight. Perhaps it was better I did it in the dark, because that way nobody could see how badly my hands were trembling. I made a transverse incision across the throat, sort of like for a thyroid operation, and I was able to blot the blood with gauze sponges. I could reach down and feel the thyroid gland, then see the trachea, which lay just behind it and in the center, with those little rings running around it. It was firm; I pierced it with the knife, making a crossroads cut, and I was able to slip a steel tube right into it. The old guy was still with us. I went down to the basement with my flashlight and got the generator running again. The lights in the hospital came back on, and we were able to take him into the examining room and complete that part of the job.

I had neither the equipment nor the training to repair the damage done by the bullet. The hospital in El Paso, where we usually took such patients, was a hundred miles away, and it was a drive of about an hour and a half by ambulance. I summoned one of our ambulance drivers, whose name was Woodrow Wilson. I had never seen him completely sober, and he was certainly far from it this evening. Fortunately, he had pretty good reflexes and managed to get by, but this night he started off creeping along at thirty-five miles per hour. It looked like it was going to be a very long trip. I cursed and said, "Woody, please hurry it up!" The next thing I knew we were doing a hundred miles per hour on a winding road heading down out of the mountains. I made Woody stop. He got in back with the patient and used the Ambu-bag to breathe for him, and I drove the rest of the way.

The neurosurgeon in El Paso operated on our patient and patched him all up. The chief had done on himself a nice prefrontal lobotomy. When the old man came back to us, he had forgotten every word of English he had ever known, spoke only Apache, and seemed extremely happy.

"THE GRASS WAS YOUNG and I was horseback. A thunderstorm was coming from where the sun goes down, and just as I was riding into the woods along a creek I saw a bird sitting on a limb. This was not a dream; it happened. I was going to shoot at the bird with the bow my grandfather made. But the bird spoke to me, saying, 'Look and listen! A voice is calling to you.' I looked up at the clouds, and I listened to the voice. Many men were coming there headfirst like arrows slanting down, and as they came they sang a sacred song and the thunder was like drumming. The song of the clouds and the voices of the men and the call of the bird were all one thing, one voice, and it said to me,

'Behold, a sacred one is calling you—
All over the sky a voice is calling!'

I sat there in a spell of wonder. The voice was coming from the place where the universe was born. And when the voice was very close to me it wheeled about toward where the sun goes down. The rain came with a big wind and a roaring. The only thing I could understand was the cry of the messenger bird.

I did not tell this to anyone. I liked to think about it, but I was afraid to tell it."

—Black Elk

W▲ ▲ ▲ ▲ ▲ ▲ ▲ ▲ ▲ ▲ ▲ ▲ ▲ ▲ ▲ ▲ ▲ ▲ ▲ ▲
E WERE AT WAR in Vietnam. In May of 1971
I hadn't received a draft notice; Uncle Sam had already
gotten his quota of docs. I was finishing up my internship
and wanted to be a surgeon. Investigating my options, I
found that I could work with the Public Health Service in
Alaska, which sounded awfully cold. But there was an open
slot in New Mexico, which sounded a lot warmer. So I
grabbed it. For two years I'd be a medicine man for a small
tribe of Apaches.

On the drive down from Albuquerque I looked out at
the dry, flat, ugly land; it seemed to me like a little south-
western Appalachia, with barbed-wire fences and cardboard
shacks here and there in a huge expanse of reddish-brown

earth. Two gaunt cows huddled at a stagnant water hole.
I felt I was going to the end of the world; it was incredibly
hot, and my Chevy didn't have air-conditioning. In that
dry, desolate land nothing interrupted or dominated the
view, it was just low-growing mesquite and prickly-pear
cactus. There were, however, great varieties of light; the
early-morning yellow in Albuquerque, where I had picked
up my papers from the Indian Health Service, now gave
way to a lovely late-afternoon violet that magically changed
the landscape. About fifty miles north of my destination I
ran into the malpais, a huge lava field with big cinder-black
rocks stretching as far as I could see. Then, off in the
distance, a mountain range, Sierra Blanca on the left, snow-
capped, 12,000 feet; on my right, Trinity, where they exploded the first atomic bomb. Continuing south, you can
actually walk out onto the desert and pick up little pieces
of green glass, which are the solidified silicates from all the
sand that melted from the terrific heat of the blast. Farther
south White Sands, a sea of gypsum, thirty miles long and
ten miles wide; some of the dunes were fifty feet high.
When the sun sets on those snowlike white hills it tints the
sands with gold; it is especially beautiful because the far-
off mountains are blue and purple. It is all trackless; the
wind breathes across the sand. As it says on the license
plates, New Mexico is the "Land of Enchantment." A year
later I would return to this desolate place with a woman I
loved very much, and she would tell me a legend about the
ghost of an Indian maiden whose husband-to-be got lost in
these great shifting hills of white sand. "Look, Jim," said
Annie, and suddenly pointed. "Pavlo Blanco!" For a moment I thought I did see it. I really did think I saw a dust
devil in the shape of a woman standing at the crest of a

dune. Dressed in her wedding gown, the woman seemed
to be searching, staring into the shadows. And then she
disappeared. The wind rippled the dune.

On first arrival, though, I doggedly kept going, to Tularosa, then turned east and back a little north. Gradually
the landscape changed into rich forested land, like the Pacific Northwest, like Washington or Oregon, green velvet
mountainsides of piñon and ponderosa pine, juniper, aspen
and oak and spruce and Douglas fir, mountain streams,
wild turkey and deer. It was a treacherous stretch of road,
and there was a big sign, "SLOW DOWN, DEATH AHEAD," over
a crude drawing of a skull with a warbonnet on it.

Finally I arrived in Mescalero (named, I think, after the
mescal plant). I had been told that over a thousand Apaches
lived there. But where were they? It was only a tiny wide
spot in the road, a few ramshackle houses and adobe huts,
falling-down trailers, a decrepit general store. I didn't see
a single soul. The white clapboard hospital was locked up,
both the front door and the emergency entrance in back. I
stood there alone, bewildered, in the dust and the heat. I
heard my voice whisper, "Hello?"

PART ONE

M▲ ▲
Y VERY FIRST PATIENT in our little
twenty-five-bed hospital was a stolid, extremely inebriated,
and very nasty Apache who had several cuts that needed
suturing. While I treated him he abused the nurses with
obscenities. (Later I learned that most of our nurses were
Pueblos, and they looked down on our patients, who were
all Apaches—the atmosphere was frequently tense and un-
pleasant.) This Apache really let loose on our head nurse,
Pita, he actually spit at her. So after having stitched the
bastard up, I grabbed him by the belt and the scruff of his
neck, took him to the front door, and deposited him gently
outside. I was rather proud of myself. Then I went back

into the hospital, where I saw Pita looking at me oddly. She said, "That was a very stupid thing to do."

I said, "Why? He was so awful to us. I don't think we should have to put up with that."

She said, "He's bad criminal. Just got released from federal penitentiary. He spent a year there."

"Well, if he only spent a year, then he couldn't have done anything that bad."

Pita said, "He had a disagreement with his brother and shot him dead."

I was a little taken aback. I said, "You get only one year in the federal penitentiary for murdering your brother?"

She said, "That's sort of the maximum no matter what you do here."

I realized I had a lot to learn (and kept a wary eye out to see if I crossed that s.o.b.'s path again).

When hunting season arrived, almost every Indian family got a deer, and they depended on the meat during the winter. Our hospital cook, a lovely Navajo lady whose husband had died long ago, said that she would be so happy to have a deer for the winter, but this year she hadn't found anybody to get her one. I had never hunted before in my life and had had minimal practice with a rifle in ROTC when I was in college, but without a second's hesitation I found myself saying, "Well, I will go out and get you a deer."

When clinic hours were over for the afternoon I hopped into that trusty '65 Chevy I had bought from a college kid back in Syracuse; I didn't even stop to change my Public

Health Service uniform (a navy uniform, since the PHS is a branch of the Coast Guard). With a 30/06 in the trunk, I hurried out to survey the surrounding hills. The eastern side of the reservation was opened up to Texans, who loved to hunt, so all the deer would run to the western side, where the hospital was, and they were plentiful. I drove ten miles up a winding dirt road between two small mountains. Lo and behold, I spied a big mule deer buck that looked like he weighed about 250 pounds standing on a hill about sixty yards away. I hopped out of the car, grabbed my gun, got the deer in my sights, though he was sort of hidden behind brush, and blasted away. I immediately thought, "Oh my God, I've wounded that deer—I'm going to have to chase him all over creation, and I am going to feel guilty as hell." I walked slowly up the hill, through all the bushes, and found that I had indeed hit him, right in the vital spot, through his aorta. There he was, dead, all 250 pounds of him. Mule deer are a little bigger than our eastern whitetail. A good hour later, in the dark, my uniform all torn and filthy, I had finally dragged the deer down to my Chevy. Without cleaning him, I stuffed him in the backseat, half into the front, his forelegs hanging out the window, and drove to the cook's house, dragged him out of the car and up onto her porch. This was a grand success and established me as a real hunter. I even received a dressed-out hind-quarter from the very appreciative cook. My standing with the nurses and hospital staff was now a little bit higher.

The very next night an Apache woman who had had many babies before, and didn't waste much time in having them, was about to deliver another. It was a hundred-yard dash from my little government-issue house to the hospital.

Unfortunately, at the corner of the hospital I ran around there was a big thornbush. I got around the sucker all right, but one of the thorns caught me in the nose like a steel hook, so that by the time I arrived to deliver this baby, which was very close to being delivered on its own, a copious flow of blood was dripping down over my mouth and chin. I pumped the soap bottle, broke it in the process, and cut a chunk out of my thumb. I looked a lot worse than the expectant mother. But I was able to deliver the baby, a fine, furiously squalling Apache boy. I cleaned everything up, including myself; with Pita's expert assistance, I got eight stitches in my thumb and called it a night.

The Pueblo Nation is spread all over northern New Mexico and Arizona; they make pottery and go on living, somehow, in our twentieth-century world. They send more of their children to school than the Apaches do. The Navajos are an even bigger and entirely different tribe; staying close to their hogans, they seldom seek medical attention, and they have an especially severe problem with tuberculosis. The Navajos are peaceful shepherds, not raiders like the Apaches. Word seeped down to us in Mescalero that up at the hospital in Shiprock they were having an epidemic of bubonic plague. They needed emergency help, and I was flown up there in a BIA Piper Cub. A bunch of prairie dogs carried a particularly virulent form of the bacteria that caused the plague, and it made big blue boils appear all over the patients before they died. The bubonic plague was what wiped out so much of medieval Europe. Now eight cases had been reported. Even in 1971, in the era of anti-biotics, if you didn't get to the afflicted in time there was really nothing you could do. We administered massive doses of streptomycin and tetracycline. I was on duty in the Ship-rock emergency room when a Navajo was brought in with respiratory arrest. I gave mouth-to-mouth and pumped on his chest and applied electrodes to shock him back into the world of the living. But it was to no avail; the Navajo died. A postmortem was done fairly quickly, and the man was found to have pneumonic plague, the same as bubonic plague except that the germ is in the lungs. It is a diffuse pneumonia, almost 100 percent fatal, and extremely con-tagious. I sweated bullets, and took I.M. streptomycin and tetracycline in massive doses. Somehow I didn't catch it. And finally they sent me back to Mescalero. I had survived the incubation period, and the epidemic was dwindling.

One night around 2:00 A.M. I was called in to treat a young Apache male, desperately uncomfortable, who was suffering from a problem I had never encountered before. I am pretty sure that at that time I had never seen an electric vibrator; I was naive about sexual toys and appliances. Here, seated in our emergency room (sort of seated, for most of his weight was supported by his hands tightly clenching the sides of the examining table), this wincing brave told me what had happened. He and his girlfriend had decided to have a little midnight fun, and during it he had her push a large vibrator up his anus. It must have been very stim-ulating because the vibrator slipped out of her grasp and disappeared into his rectum. They couldn't get it back out. The poor guy's ass was still humming away. I went to work, but there seemed to be no way I or any of my tools could bring it out. I really didn't want to send him, ass abuzz, all the way down that long bumpy road to El Paso.

After nearly an hour's work, he was so traumatized that I had to give him general anesthesia, under which the anus can be dilated up to a reasonable size. Finally I was able to grasp hold of the vibrator and extract it. The thing looked a little like a fish, bravely wiggling in my hand.

"WHISKEY AND WINE are the most terrible things the white man ever brought to the Indian people. Alcohol is the bitterest curse we have, and it has done more to weaken and destroy us than anything else."

—Frank Fool's Crow

▌▲ ▲ ▲ ▲ ▲ ▲ ▲ ▲ ▲ ▲ ▲ ▲ ▲ ▲ ▲ ▲ ▲ ▲ ▲ ▲

T WAS A PRETTY QUIET LIFE. I spent
my evenings reading, mainly medical journals, and watching junk on TV. Once in a while I'd go down to the PX
at Holloman Air Force Base, a forty-five-minute drive. I
tried duck hunting and bagged some greasy little ducks,
which even with my special sauce *à l'orange* were too tough
to eat. I threw them into my double-size government-issue
freezer in the garage along with that hindquarter of deer.

In the middle of the night I was called to deliver Maude
Big Foot's fifth child. Maude was a fine strong woman, and
I'd gotten to know her during her several visits to the
prenatal clinic. It looked like a simple delivery. She was
effacing fast, I was sure I'd be back in bed within the hour.

I examined her a second time, and a gush of blood came out like a geyser.

I had taken the usual two-month rotation in obstetrics during my internship, had delivered lots of babies, even a breach, and had learned how to use low forceps. We'd been cautioned about placenta previa. All docs are terrified of it. The placenta can attach itself to the cervix, and when the cervix dilates and you reach in there with your finger you may puncture a mass of arteries and veins, and the patient will bleed to death in minutes. You *must* do a C-section immediately or lose both mother and baby.

I stared at that gush of blood and the rapidly dying mother. I was unable to move. Frozen to the spot. I'd seen a C-section, but never had done one. A soft firm voice said, "Doctor, here's the knife, I'll scrub her abdomen with Betadine." Annie Mendez, the night nurse, put the knife in my hand, guided me to the left side of the table, splashed Betadine on Maude's large belly, and I plunged the knife in, cutting from umbilicus to pubis. Then a similar cut into the uterus. I pulled out the baby and peeled out the pulsing placenta. Annie calmly hung up the saline, shot in the Pitocin and ergonovine to make the uterus contract, Maude stopped bleeding, and the baby squalled. I'd done it, thanks to Annie. Sewing up was easy, and I was even able to give the new mother a little Demerol; she'd not let out a whimper, and I'd not had time even to think of anesthesia, much less give it.

Annie Mendez was an extremely smart nurse. Her black eyes and high cheekbones were pure Indian, and her jet-black hair cascaded down her back. She was half Lakota and half Sioux; when she was a girl her name was Annie Messenger Bird. She had two ex-husbands—one of whom she was technically still married to—and she had a teenage son, Silas, whom she adored. What I liked most about her, aside from her wonderful laugh, was her uncanny ability to soothe scared people. She had a terrific way with our patients, who would often ask specifically for her and would even wait until nightfall to come in (Annie had a day job in Tularosa as a high-school history teacher).

She had pulled me through that emergency C-section —mother, baby, and doctor all made it. Annie intervened again one night when I did my usual run down to the house to read Key and Conwell (the orthopedic text). A big husky Indian was patiently waiting in the X-ray room for me to relocate his dislocated shoulder. I was about to do the Kocher maneuver, which is fine in expert hands, but the inexperienced can easily break the arm that way. Annie simply said, "Let's give him some Demerol and let him lie down first." I nodded, she gave the Demerol and had the patient lie on his stomach with the dislocated-shoulder arm hanging down, and in it popped.

Annie had a master's degree in social work from the University of New Mexico, four hours away in Albuquerque, and she asked me to look at her thesis, "Alcohol Policy on Indian Reservations." She had done an enormous amount of research, and I found her arguments extremely interesting. As everybody knows, you can't talk about Indians without talking about alcohol. Many experts think that Indians have a genetic disability to metabolize alcohol. Native Americans have the highest rate of alcoholism in the world, and a rate of alcoholic cirrhosis eighteen times that of non-Indians. At Mescalero, 60 percent of our budget was for alcohol-related injuries and illnesses.

The conclusion of Annie's thesis addressed the question

of whether it was good medical policy to keep the reservations "dry." In 1953 the tribes themselves had acquired the power to define the provisions of alcohol prohibition, and one-third of all reservations had legalized it. At ours, the president of the tribal council, Barnabas Lester, could have ruled either way. Chief Lester had said, "I am an ordained minister, and have never had drink in my life. I am also a politician. I will abide by the results of a referendum."

Annie came down unequivocally on the side of "wet." Access to alcohol, she argued, was not stopped by prohibition. All it did was lead to widespread bootlegging. And this contrived access meant increased dysfunctional drinking—rapid drinking, binge drinking, drunk driving. (Pathetic little white crosses and small shrines on the sides of the highway to the north and south of Mescalero were eloquent testimonials.) Annie pointed out that only one tribe out of ninety-two had returned to prohibition after having legalized alcohol. Her thesis compared three "wet" tribes with four "dry" ones: over a decade, those with legalized alcohol had significantly lower mortality rates for cirrhosis, lower rates of motor vehicle crashes, only half the number of suicides, significantly lower homicide rates. Annie's point was that legalization of alcohol leads to less-abusive consumption. The one reservation that had repealed its legalization was the Oglala Sioux at Pine Ridge—but arrests of Indians during the two legalization months were a third fewer than during the same months of the year before and the year after.

One night when our shift was over I invited Annie to my little house for a cup of coffee and a talk about her thesis. One aspect of it troubled me, and I said so right away. When you legalize booze you make it socially okay. You sanction it. And I hated it, really hated it, when I had to treat an eleven-year-old girl who was obviously drunk. I hated it even more when I knew that a few years later I would have to deliver her damaged baby, which would never have a shot at a full life because mother had boozed all through her pregnancy.

When I glumly delivered myself of these notions, a wonderful little drama played itself out on Annie Mendez's face. A three-act drama, at least. In act one she was mad, and I thought to myself, "Well, this very pretty Indian lady does not take too well to criticism." Act two was a combination of surprise and hurt; she looked a little lost, with a funny glance upward, a roll of her eyes, as if this were an old story, as if she were once again being tested on something she hadn't studied for. The third act began when I mentioned the eleven-year-old girl and then her baby; Annie Mendez got very sad, her eyes full of woe; but at the same time she was suddenly looking at me, too, as if she were seeing me for the first time. Both our voices immediately became quieter. Years later I would remember and treasure that moment. It was so peculiar—there we were discussing a desperate social and medical problem, trying to make sense of its terror and weight, its probable cause and possible cure. Yet the moment was so oddly sexual.

Annie was thinking of something, however, and she emitted a little sigh of resignation. "All our land has been stolen. What the hell does that do to your self-esteem?"

I whispered to my coffee cup, "You mean that despair is a cause of poor health."

"Yes," she said, "I do mean that, honey."

The word "honey" made me look at her again. And she was looking right back at me, real hard. She took a breath and said, "They call us 'prairie niggers.' There's a sign in a Ruidoso bar, 'No Dogs or Indians Allowed.'" Then, a little irritated with herself, "Sorry. I talk too much."

I said, "But you don't talk like an Indian."

She just kept looking at me. "What do you think an Indian talks like?"

"Oh, come on, you know what I mean."

"You mean I don't say 'How!' or 'Long time no see'?"

"Give me a break."

"'No can do.' There, is that better?"

"Jesus!"

She paused. Not looking at me, she said softly, "It's my heritage, not my culture."

I nodded, as if I knew what the hell that meant.

"I grew up—insofar as I can lay claim to having grown up—in a foster home."

Again I nodded.

"I was the only Indian in the whole school. Grammar school. High school. Even college. I guess my whole life has been a struggle to come back to my people—to come back to my real home. But my white dad and my white mom were terrific. Dad was a wonderful guy. Civil rights lawyer. I adored him. Except for one terrible mistake."

"What was that?"

"Oh—" She looked wildly around, as if for an intruder. "Haven't you got anything to *drink?*"

I did have a pint of Jack Daniels. I went and got it and poured her a stiff shot. She swigged it down in silence. Then she told me a little about her day job, teaching history at Tularosa High School. She talked about the Anglo cowboys, with their big boots and Stetsons, the guys who drove pickups with rifles slung behind the back windows. Their hero was Barry Goldwater, and they hated "government interference." Their parents had put up all the "Impeach Earl Warren" signs, parents who held seats on the school board and were worried that Annie was teaching positive views of communism. In her class on comparative theories of government, the superintendent of schools had come and sat in back to see if Annie was "quoting the party line." Kids would come into class in the afternoon, after having heard Paul Harvey on the radio, and they'd spout his opinions.

"So," I said, "you hate them."

"Oh, no," she said quickly. "I'm *fond* of them. They're extremely likable—open, direct, lots of fun. I mean, well, I'm not *happy* that they say 'DWI' means 'Driving While Indian.' And it's dangerous when Anglo girls date Indian guys. Lots of scuffles in the halls. The Indian kids are bused in the twenty miles in the morning, bused back the twenty miles after classes—they hardly ever get involved in student activities."

I reached out and put my white hand on her dark one. I patted it. Her silver ring, the turquoise stone.

She didn't seem to notice my hand. She mentioned that one of her students had made a lovely mistake on his last paper (and it took me a moment, for some reason, to get it): the boy had written about "this doggity dog world of ours."

Annie laughed. A big, goofball laugh. And then she tossed back another shot of whiskey and talked about Charles "Chuck" Warhurst, the football coach, who was afraid his players would flunk her course in American history. At noon Chuck would get into his car, drive around, drink a pint of vodka. When he came back at one o'clock he was pretty loose tongued. He was very concerned about one of his players, Calvin. "And so was I," Annie said. "I put Calvin adjacent to my desk. Where I could touch him. Calvin would put his head down on his desk, his head in the crook of his elbow, and he'd just *stare*. Then, one day—I still don't know how it happened—Calvin was sitting up straight, his hand went up, he answered questions perfectly, showed thorough knowledge of everything we'd covered."

"How'd you do it?"

"I don't *know*. I wish the hell I did. So I could do it again."

I sat there in my chair and looked at her. Somehow I felt that way back deep in her past this woman had been badly harmed, terribly disappointed. And here she sat now in my stupid PHS cottage, a drunk Indian lady whose master's thesis was on alcohol abuse.

I said, "I thought your thesis was very persuasive."

She shook her head, but she was smiling in a conspiratorial way.

"Excuse me?"

"Oh, nothing," she said. "I just remember when my son was about ten, maybe eleven years old. One night he saw me all dressed up to go out on a date. My precocious little Silas said to me, 'Mom, don't you think that blouse is a little persuasive?' " Annie laughed again. "He meant to say 'provocative.' "

I nodded.

Around two-thirty she said she had to go.

I said I'd drive her.

"No, Jimbo," she said. "The cops won't stop me. I got Daddy Warbucks."

"Daddy War—?"

"Poppa Daddy. Or would you like me to say, 'Heap Big Chief'?"

"Oh. Barnabas Lester." I peered at her. "You're—friends?"

She laughed again. "He's my father-in-law."

Oh. Oh?

"Silas's grandfather."

"Well, whatever your connections, lady, I don't want you on the road." I turned her around and marched her into my bedroom. "You can crash here." I sat her on the bed, took off her shoes, pulled her legs up, and made her lie down.

"Oh, God," she said.

I leaned over and gave her a good-night peck on the cheek. I drew back a little, looking at her. I hadn't had any sex at all since I had arrived at this place. And Annie, through her fog, sensed my feelings. With a grin she was wide-awake, and she shook her finger at me. "Don't even *think* about it!"

▪ ▲
DID, THOUGH. Who knows, really, what had brought me to this forlorn precinct of the planet? I had come, that's all. And I had found this remarkable woman who taught history by day and was a nurse at night. More and more now at the hospital we sought each other out. Whenever we had time for a coffee break we'd talk awhile, usually about medical matters, but sometimes to share personal stuff. Early on I found out what her adoptive father's terrible mistake had been. Only, Annie wasn't sure that it really was a mistake. For many years the man had lived with cancer; through proper medication it had been kept in remission. He never told his adopted little Indian princess. Didn't want to cloud her childhood and adolescence.

Only when the therapy was no longer adequate and the disease went out of control did he sit down and tell her. Three months later he was dead. And to this day Annie felt a vague sense of betrayal, mixed in with loss and grief. If only she had *known*, she said, if only her dad had believed in her enough, believed that she was able to handle his suffering, to help him through it, if only . . .

She asked me about my father. I sighed. What's to say? Pop was, well, I suppose one could say he wasn't emotionally very expressive. "I discovered that," I said, smiling, "when he broke my heart by saying, 'You're too old to kiss.' I was seven." And, oddly enough, there had been a cancer secret in my childhood, too. Only it was Mom. One day when I was in eighth grade my father took me aside and said, "Never will we mention in this house the word 'cancer.' " Mom, an extremely superstitious person, went crazy even at the mention of the word. She thought "cancer" was God's way of telling you you had done something terribly wrong with your life—cancer was your own doing. So my father and I maintained the fiction, right up to her death; the Men in the Family never said the word "cancer."

Annie's resiliency and her gift for laughter kept us from moaning and groaning like that all the time. We exchanged lots of little jokes, and we got into the habit of touching each other whenever we'd meet. Just a pat. And when our shifts were over we'd chat out in the parking lot. Kissing good-night, though, she'd always avert her lips, offering me her cheek. Finally, one dark morning before sunrise, I blurted out, "When do I get a *real* kiss?"

She stared down at the ground. "I know. Yes. I'm not being—coy. I'm—oh, Jimmy, I'm sorry. I'm just—"

"Okay," I said. "It's your call."

"Thank you," she said. And when she looked up at me she had tears in her eyes.

But what an extraordinary nurse! Best I've ever worked with. Once, a guy came in who had swallowed a toothpick. The damn things don't show up on an X ray, of course, being wood, and you never know where the hell they've gone. They disappear into the small intestinal tract, get hung up, and gradually burrow through the wall of the bowel, which causes a local infection. Or sometimes they perforate something and end up in the damnedest places—they work their way into a vein, and they have even been found embedded in the heart. Any number of reports cite deaths of people who have swallowed toothpicks, so it is absolutely key to grab the little suckers before they get out of the stomach. You have to be careful if the patients have just had a big meal (which they usually have, hence the toothpick), because if they vomit and you've got them sedated, they can aspirate, which could be fatal.

I was lucky to have a flexible end-vision gastroscope. The cost of sending people off to Roswell with foreign bodies in their stomachs had prompted Chief Lester to make sure the Indian Health Service supplied our small hospital with a gastroscope, a recent innovation. Now, looking down this guy with my scope, I saw mouthfuls of meat and pieces of corn on the cob and baked potato, but I was not able to find the toothpick. I was standing there, trying to figure out how to do this guy, when Annie said, "Why don't we pour a cup of black coffee down him through the gastroscope?" Sure, I thought, why not? So we filled him up. Then I looked down again, through the scope, and there

floating on a little black lake of coffee was our white toothpick. I snared it.

If you ask a doctor what good nursing is, you are likely
to hear, "I don't know, I never watch 'em." But I watched
Annie and saw her literally talk patients through their injury or illness. For all the years since Clara Barton, nurses
have been known as "angels of mercy." And, by God, Annie
was one. I'd stare at a patient's chart, look at the lab work,
think about the disease, but Annie would think about the
patient—about the patient's family, comfort, morale, about
providing an extra back rub, special foods, words of encouragement.

The oldest woman I have ever seen, tiny Lucy Blackfoot
(she was a hundred, anyway), showed up one night in the
ER with two ice-cold blue legs. She had no groin pulses.
That was easy to figure out: she'd thrown a clot from the
heart that had blocked the circulation of both legs. This
was really too much for me to handle, and I sent her to El
Paso, where they fished out the clot. Then, uh-oh, the hole
that had been made in the axillary artery closed up. So they
went back to the operating room and fixed it. The vascular
surgeon in El Paso could not believe Lucy Blackfoot had
pulled through all this, but she had, and they sent her back
to us as soon as possible.

Then Lucy began to experience a whole host of problems. I would deal with them one after another: she had
bad heart pain and angina, she got shocky and looked like
she was surely going to die. I put her on all the appropriate
medicines, tried everything I could think of, but she went
into shock again, which damaged her liver and almost shut
down her kidneys. After six weeks of hospitalization, she

was just dwindling away, and her neighbor was coming in every day to ask me why I was prolonging this proud old lady's suffering. Finally Annie told me she had had a long, long talk with Lucy Blackfoot. Lucy was afraid she'd never go back home to her little farm, she'd be put in a nursing home, and she'd rather die than have that happen. So the next morning on my rounds I told Lucy that the plan was for her to go home if only I could get her to perk up a little. Boy, did Lucy perk up! In one week that frail, ancient little woman was out of the hospital, and Annie arranged home care for her.

It sounds corny, but I am absolutely convinced that encouragement like that, attentive and careful kindness to the patient, gets a lot of people out of the hospital and back to their lives. Good nurses do that. Annie was without professional inhibitions and felt quite free to correct me or suggest things I hadn't thought of. She was bright as hell, compassionate, innovative, a troubleshooter, soothing to patient and doctor alike. She had a wonderful sense of humor about herself: on a coffee break, she told me that her students at the high school took a great deal of interest in the clothes she wore and were eager to suggest ways in which she might improve her appearance. One morning, when she went into the classroom wearing a pair of slacks and a sweater, a boy said to her, "You ought to dress like that more often. You dress too *old*—it would do wonders if you'd dress your age." Annie always spent a lot of time in class working at the big maps, pointing out faraway places, and she noticed that the guys would look at her feet. Eventually she found out that they didn't like her opaque, thick support stockings—so they took up a collection and gave her a little anonymous gift, a pair of new nylons. Whenever she'd tell me stories like that she'd blush a little and deliver the punch line with her great half-knowing, half-baffled laugh.

Christ, I found myself trailing her around like a goddamn puppy, just to be near her. She told me about an eleven-year-old Apache girl, the younger sister of one of her students at Tularosa High, who was hanging around her, a kind of schoolgirl crush. One day Annie couldn't find her wristwatch, she had last seen it on her desk; she searched everywhere, at home, school, and the hospital. Finally she asked the girl if she had any idea where the watch might be. "Oh, no," the girl said, very slowly and intensely. "I have *no* idea where it could be." And the girl didn't come around for several days. Then Annie showed me an unsigned note, printed, that she had received:

If you are looking for your watch you will find it hanging on a bush near your house where Silas shoot his bow and arrow.

And sure enough, Annie found it there.

I have no idea why that simple little story made such an impression on me, but I found myself thinking about it, playing with it, visualizing the exact moment when Annie spotted the watch on the bush. I hadn't met Annie's son, Silas, but that night in my dreams Silas was there, with his bow and arrow, hunting deer, providing for the old spirit woman, Lucy Blackfoot.

▲ ▲ ▲ ▲ ▲ ▲ ▲ ▲ ▲ ▲ ▲ ▲ ▲ ▲ ▲ ▲ ▲ ▲ ▲ ▲

T SADDENED ME to see how few of the people actually worked. There was certainly adequate land to be farmed, timber to be cut, mines to be mined, and a ski resort to be run. But, as Annie said, the Mescalero Apaches had been raiders for centuries until we blundered in and stuck them on a reservation. Some of the men had acquired considerable fame by being fire fighters, and had been shipped all over the country whenever there was a big fire to fight. They were quite good at it, and later in my stay I had the opportunity to see them in action; they were very impressive. But the only real contact I had with the Mescaleros was at the hospital, which had one wing for the men (we called it "the bullpen") and one for the women.

It had been built in 1913, when the Chiricahua Apaches were released from Fort Sill in Oklahoma (where they had been classified as "prisoners of war") and came here to live with the Mescaleros.

I continued to annoy and disappoint myself with the mistakes I made in the clinic. A woman came in holding in her arms a little baby wrapped in a blanket. I asked the mother a bunch of questions—is the baby off its feed, does the baby seem less active, has the baby's stool changed? Then I said I had to take a look at the baby. Mother said it was asleep. I said that I really did have to examine it. So finally she parted with the baby, and it seemed to be an extremely sound sleeper; I tried to wake it, again tried to wake it, and suddenly to my horror I realized it was dead. (Actually, technically it was alive, it was completely stiff with meningitis; I tore around, gave it a spinal tap, gave it massive doses of antibiotics, everything I could think of, but it was no use, and the infant died in a matter of hours.) The next day another woman came in with a little baby wrapped in a blanket; we went through the same routine questions, and all at once I thought to myself, "Jesus! I have the same tragedy on my hands," so I quickly grabbed the baby out of the woman's arms and really shook it, and the baby naturally let out a scream of outrage, and its mother looked at me with an expression of "What on earth is this crazy doctor doing to my kid?"

I had to work only one month with the doctor I was replacing. Thank God, for I took an instant dislike to Winston. Winston E. Cunningham. He was intent on getting out of the Indian Service and on with his training in gynecology. He'd landed in Mescalero two years before, when all the docs were drafted or went into the Public Health

Service. Evidently he'd made it clear from day one that he was above all this mundane business of taking care of sick Indians. He was usually slumped behind his desk, and the nurses would parade the patients in front of him, mention the symptoms, and he'd dole out some penicillin tabs. He rarely touched a patient, much less examined one. However, at times he would arouse from his torpor, come around the desk, and shoo the nurses away. This was when the patient was a lovely young woman.

It was only after he was gone that Annie told me of his more sinister side. Apparently Winston would tell young women that they had herpes simplex and that their babies would be born blind. But, Winston said, he had "special access" to a "special vaccine"; he said that the vaccine had to be used right at the time of intercourse. He screwed them right on the X-ray table. And then gave them this "special vaccine." Winston E. Cunningham. But sexual abuse was pretty much par for the course in the white man's treatment of Indians; there seemed to be an enormous amount of child sexual abuse in BIA boarding schools, most of it unreported; when reported, unremedied.

It was the children, the children most of all, who drove me to despondency. One night while on call I picked up the phone, and a tiny voice asked if I could come see his little brother, who seemed to be very, very sick. I drove along a dirt road with shabby little houses on both sides, a few broken-down pickup trucks in the yards, and found the house where the phone call had come from. Sitting by the front door were several comatose adults, and several more inside the door, but none of these were the parents of the children in the house, nor were they paying any attention to them. Five children in that one little house; the boy who had called me was six years old, and he was trying to open a can of Spam for dinner for the other four children, all younger than he. The three-year-old was the one that the boy was so concerned about; this youngster was very dehydrated, had a bad ear infection and a temperature of 105 degrees. A four-year-old brother and a two-year-old sister were relatively okay. As I was gathering up the children and putting them in the car, the six-year-old said, "Don't forget my little sister," and lying there in a corner of the house on an old blanket, and covered by nothing else, was a one-month-old infant girl, also severely ill with dehydration. She looked like she had not had anything to eat for some time. What usually happened was that the parents left on Friday for a weekend drinking binge, and when Sunday night rolled around we would start seeing these infants and young children in terrible shape.

The BIA, three hundred miles north in Albuquerque, didn't want to hear about such problems. They rarely drove down to see what we were doing. So long as we weren't bankrupting the system, so long as the reports were reasonably okay, they let us alone. Stock the pharmacy, pay the nurses and maintenance men, patch people up the best we could. And the Indians who came in usually had one of only a few things wrong with them—they either had an injury or they had an infection, gallstones, or cirrhosis. I saw very little cancer. That was mainly because they didn't live long enough—the median death age was thirty-nine. Or if they did contract cancer they'd creep off to their own medicine man and die, without ever seeing us.

Some of those people's secrets were passed on to me by the other doctor I worked with, Max Rubenstein, whom I was fond of immediately. Tall and skinny, with a shock of red hair and beautiful green eyes, Max had an oddly endearing effeminacy about him. And a razor wit. I had noticed among the Apache men that they usually looked at me strangely when we shook hands. Max explained it to me—he said that in my effort to counter my status as an ineffectual eastern city boy I had been rather too hearty in my manly handshakes. Apaches don't do it that way. They barely touch. The handshake is almost limp, a gentle brush, hand to hand, and it means "You are my friend." What I thought of as a masculine grip meant to them "I'm mad at you." Max explained that to me, and he taught me so many other things—how pregnant women can't go to funerals, the meaning of the bright little scarfs on the cradle boards to ward off the evil eye.

One night over a glass of wine (Max called it *Château de Bubba*), he got pissed off at me for referring to the "race" of our patients. "They're not a *race*," he said.

"They're not?"

"No," Max said. "They're an ecosystemic people."

I looked at him. "It'll never catch on."

Although we quickly passed to another subject, that "race" business kept percolating on a back burner in my mind. And I broke out, "Do you object to 'race' because it goes back to when the Mongols crossed over from Siberia to the North American continent—"

Max pulled himself up to his considerable height and shook his finger in my face. "Listen, before you talk that crap you better get your Bering Straight!"

Max had had four years of residency and was in Mescalero on the Berry plan: the government had paid for the residency in surgery, and now Max owed them that time back. He had been sent to Mescalero because Barnabas

Lester had pulled more than a few strings to get us upgraded
to a hospital with an operating room. We were extremely
lucky to have Max, extremely lucky to have a well-equipped
operating room, a good nurse anesthesiologist, and a blood
bank, all rarities in most reservation hospitals. Max was
superb in most aspects of general surgery, comfortable with
lung surgery and vascular surgery, but he hated neurosurgery and avoided it at all costs. (I think he had seen too
many "vegetables" on his service during his residency.) He
planned to return for two or three additional years in cardiac
surgery after he got his bill paid. He wasn't required to be
in Mescalero all the time, so every other night he might
disappear, who knows where, and when I was on call he
usually wasn't around to help.

But Max was just terrific. One day we had a tough,
lanky, rather old Indian come in with jaundice. This man
was absolutely yellow. We did the usual lab work and
suspected that he had a common-bile-duct stone (there was
a very high incidence of gallstones), but we were bothered
by his having no pain. Painless jaundice? Also, he was a
little anemic. Max went in to remove the gallbladder and
explored the common bile duct. Much to his dismay, he
found a firm golf-ball-sized tumor in the head of the pancreas. Pancreatic cancer is almost 100 percent lethal, and
the standard of the day was to hook the gallbladder to the
intestine so that the patient wouldn't become totally jaun-
diced. But Max decided to do a Whipple, a herculean procedure that would give the patient his only chance for
survival. Max cut out half of the guy's stomach; then, after
freeing everything up, he took out all the duodenum. Next,
he cut across the pancreas just where it crosses the big vessels
that feed the intestine and liver, and he got the tumor out

with about a centimeter to spare. He meticulously hooked the remaining stomach to the intestine, then the bile duct to the intestine, and then the pancreas to the intestine. This last hookup is the most dangerous; if it leaks, it either kills the patient or causes a fistula that exudes pancreatic juice, which eats away at the abdominal skin. Max whistled through the surgery in about six hours. The patient did fine, and the pathology sections that had been sent to El Paso showed that all of the margins were clear of tumor. Our guy went home in two weeks, grumbling about how long it took white doctors to fix a little problem like jaundice. Well, it was the single most brilliant piece of surgery I'd ever seen, and it was done in a twenty-five-bed hospital on an Indian reservation.

Max Rubenstein couldn't fix everything. A little Apache boy about eight years old got hit by a Jeep at a high rate of speed and was thrown about fifty feet. Our ambulance crew picked him up off the ground, and in a case like that the crew tries not to move the person's neck or move his back, they just tie him into a stretcher and put sand blocks or head blocks around his neck to avoid further damage. The little boy was brought in in a hurry; when he arrived he was, to my eye, dead. He wasn't breathing, he was blue, and he didn't have any heart rate. I happened to be in the emergency room and got a team working on him—a little boy like that, you want to give it your best shot. When you looked at this kid you could not see any evidence of physical damage, he was just lying there blue, no head injury. I immediately intubated him and began to breathe for him, thumped on his chest, gave him adrenaline. Max made a huge slice in his chest, reached in, grabbed his heart, and began to squeeze it: immediate open-heart cardiac massage.

And the puzzling thing was that as we stood there, with Max pumping that flaccid little heart, the boy began to get a little blood pressure back, a little color in his cheeks. We figured he must have massive abdominal bleeding and had bled out during that short period of time (there can be such sheer effect that the aorta will break in half and the whole chest or abdomen gets crammed full of blood). So he was taken immediately to the operating room. When Max opened him up, we realized what had happened. It was a catastrophic wound; all of this boy's abdominal organs had been blown out the back and were just lying there: a couple of kidneys, intestine, part of the liver, the pancreas, all of it splashed on the cart and just lying there beneath him. Max spent over three hours pulling everything back into the boy's abdomen, putting it into place, trying to stop all the bleeding. I was awestruck by my colleague's speed and efficiency, the inventiveness of it, the daring moves; I thought while I watched that Max Rubenstein would some-day be a world-class thoracic surgeon. But suddenly, drenched with perspiration, Max stopped and tore off his mask and slumped against a wall; every miracle he had performed was to no avail, and the boy had died on the table.

T▲ ▲ ▲ ▲ ▲ ▲ ▲ ▲ ▲ ▲ ▲ ▲ ▲ ▲ ▲ ▲ ▲ ▲ ▲ ▲
HE POLITICS OF THE reservation were
pretty clear-cut. It was essentially a one-man show. The
chief, Barnabas Lester, a full-blooded Apache, was an in-
timidating figure: very tall by Apache standards (over six
feet), broad shouldered, heavyset, an extremely strong-
looking man. He had cruel eyes, almost black, still seething
with anger and disgust at the white man (although he had
had the Bureau of Indian Affairs build his house, and he
got fine brick and the best lumber and free labor, and was
the only Indian who lived in a house that by western standards would be considered palatial). He was the best-
educated Indian on the reservation; after graduating cum
laude from Dartmouth, he had gone on to seminary and

took considerable pride in being an ordained minister. He made frequent trips to Washington, and on his desk was a photograph of him with President Eisenhower. He spoke at high government levels not only for the Apaches but for all American Indians. From behind his large horn-rimmed glasses he seemed to me to look out with genuine dislike for Anglos in general and doctors in particular. He evidently had driven out two of my predecessors on some basis or other. To make matters even more difficult, his wife worked as one of the nurses in the hospital; she was a refractory woman and had to be supervised constantly. She would report back to him each evening on what she saw as our screwups.

One day in morning clinic I glanced out the window and saw a large German shepherd that was obviously in agony from a mouth full of porcupine quills. I had no idea whose dog it was, but as soon as clinic hours were over I went out and got the dog and brought it into the office. I was going to knock it out with Pentothal and remove the quills. Before I could do that, however, Barnabas Lester arrived on the scene and announced that it was his dog and he would take it home. He said he did not need any help at all. I said, "Fine," and motioned to Pita that they would be back so we might as well keep the setup ready. Sure enough, about half an hour later the chief returned, and he said that maybe he could use a little bit of help after all, the dog didn't seem to enjoy his trying to pull the quills out of its mouth. So I gave the dog the Pentothal, removed the quills, and that was that. Dogs, or at least this dog, must not be very bright, because a week later it appeared in the same condition. This time I made a house call and put the dog on the front porch and gave it more Pentothal and removed the quills again. (Incidentally, it is a good idea to cut the quills before you remove them, but unfortunately I didn't learn that lesson until after I had removed my last quill.) Afterward, Barnabas and I had some iced tea on the porch. Now I was a man of achieved status, and Barnabas shared some of his life's experiences with me. At one point he said, in his big rumbling bass voice, "As I said to Khrushchev, 'I hope you have better luck in your treaties with the United States than we did.' " He chuckled and took me inside to show off some fine crystal Khrushchev had given him.

A week or so later he came to my little house with a brown lunch sack in his hands. He thanked me again for fixing up his dog and gave me the lunch sack. It contained a Santa Clara black pot; when Max saw it on my desk he told me to hold on to it, it was quite valuable. Max peered at it and whispered quickly, "Yes!"

"So tractable, so peaceable, are these people, that I swear to your Majesties there is not in the world a better nation. They love their neighbors as themselves, and their discourse is ever sweet and gentle, and accompanied with a smile; and though it is true that they are naked, yet their manners are decorous and praiseworthy."

—Christopher Columbus to King Ferdinand
and Queen Isabella

P▲▲▲▲▲▲▲▲▲▲▲▲▲▲▲▲▲▲

ERCY TORTILLA, an old man born around the time Geronimo gave up, came in one day with a fracture of the arm; he had fallen forward on his outstretched hands, and the wrist bone had been impacted upward. You have to align such a thing correctly, or the arm and hand will never be functional again. We usually shoot some Xylocaine into the patient, and pull up and then push downward to align things; it's quite painful even with the Xylocaine, and it requires a cast for about eight weeks. Percy Tortilla didn't want the shot, and I set the bone, and I swear he never even winced. I did a real nice job; I looked at it under X-ray, and I was so pleased, the alignment looked perfect. I asked him to check back in a week. He came into town three days later for some other reason, and the cast was gone; he said he couldn't chop wood with it.

Another rather elderly gentleman known as Custer (I liked that) was a cowboy; one day he was trying to pull a bull forward by the horns into a truck, and the bull lowered its head and gored Custer in the thigh. He didn't do anything about it, and after a couple of days his leg had swollen so badly that he couldn't get his boot off. He wouldn't go down into El Paso to see a specialist, just kept demanding that we take the boot off, which we did.

These people seemed to take major catastrophes as if they were just nicks and scrapes. One night a bowlegged guy came in, who had something in his hand and couldn't talk right. In a matter-of-fact tone he said, "I os my ung." When he opened up his hand, there sat half his tongue. He'd been out with his girlfriend, and she didn't like what was going on, so she bit his tongue off, she bit it clean through. A few nights later, a woebegone little Apache had been waiting for me to come out of the ER, and when I did he asked me if I knew how to make a sling for a man's scrotum. I said, "Well, maybe." He took me out to the parking lot, where I found, lying in a beat-up old Ford, another Apache man, also woebegone, who said he had been out with a married woman, and the husband had caught 'em and knocked him out and then just sliced in and peeled his scrotum back. I asked him when this had happened, and he said it had been around noon. Now it was almost midnight. I said, "Doesn't that *hurt?*" And he said yeah.

Such stoicism always amazed me. The Apaches are not all that talkative, and I found them hard to get to know. Rufus Sundayman, my other alcoholic ambulance driver, a tough little guy, lived alone; Rufus was extremely reclusive and drank all the time, surrounded by three or four vicious dogs. He did his job sullenly and usually rather poorly; he refused to have anything to do with the modern world.

This isolation and toughness sometimes combined in sinister ways. I was on duty in the clinic when a four-year-old girl was brought in with rope burns on her tiny wrists. She was sobbing uncontrollably. Her vagina was ripped into the rectum, and her thighs and hips were badly bruised. She had been raped by her uncle. We gave her a light general anesthetic, then I examined her. It did not seem to me possible that anyone could actually have done this. I took a very long needle and stuck novocaine into the little girl's vagina and rectum; I put in suture after suture to repair the wound. Fortunately, I had had a fair amount of experience doing this with women during childbirth. It had happened on three or four occasions, and they had always healed up if proper care and attention were given. There was ground-in dirt in the wound and streaked blood on her little abdomen and running down both her skinny legs. It took a lot of time and patience to repair the recto-vaginal tear. The space in that area was hardly large enough to accommodate my finger. After I had finished, her parents told me that they had found the uncle and that they would punish him in their own way. Apparently there had been some sort of interfamily warfare going on. The uncle was known among his own people as a bad fellow, always crazed on firewater or peyote. Very few had any use for him. The little girl's father asked me not to report the case to the police, but I did, and the officers went out to track down the rapist. When they found him he was already in the custody of six of his relatives, who were waiting for day-break to march him up to a place where, when the sun was high, they would stake him out on an anthill. The officers took charge, and the uncle eventually ended up in federal court, as so many Indian matters do. I was called at the trial to testify about what the medical findings had been. There was little to say; the findings spoke for themselves.

Never before had I seen such cruelty. One day I watched four or five kids climb up onto an old horse owned by some Indian family and ride it back and forth until the animal was about to drop; the kids (who were old enough to know better) were running that poor old horse into the ground. In a little field down the road from the hospital I watched seven or eight boys tossing around an object like a football. They were having a gleeful good time of it. What they were throwing around was a little kitten, and they did so until they killed it. Some of those children's tricks were almost diabolical: teenaged boys found great sport in running around the reservation and finding a drunk passed out and lying face down on the ground; the boys would take a beer bottle, break it, and place it very carefully under the poor drunk's head so that when he moved and started to get up he would slash himself in the face.

"Such of the goshoots as we saw, along the road and hanging about the stations, were small, lean, 'scrawny' creatures; in complexion a dull black like the ordinary American negro; their faces and hands bearing dirt which they had been hoarding and accumulating for months, years, and even generations, according to the age of the proprietor; a silent, sneaking, treacherous-looking race; taking note of everything, covertly, like all the other 'Noble Red Men' that we (do not) read about, and betraying no sign in their countenances, indolent, everlastingly patient and tireless, like all other Indians; prideless beggars—for if the beggar instinct were left out of an Indian he would not 'go,' any more than a clock without a pendulum; hungry, always hungry, and yet never refusing anything that a hog would eat, though often eating what a hog would decline; hunters, but having no higher ambition than to kill and eat jackass-rabbits, crickets, and grasshoppers, and embezzle carrion from the buzzards and coyotes; savages who, when asked if they have the common Indian belief in a Great Spirit, show a something which almost amounts to emotion, thinking whiskey is referred to; a thin, scattering race of almost naked black children, these Goshoots are, who produce nothing at all, and have no villages, and no gatherings together into strictly defined tribal communities—a people whose only shelter is a rag cast on a bush to keep off a portion of the snow, and yet who inhabit one of the most rocky, wintry, repulsive wastes that our country or any other can exhibit.

The Bushmen and our Goshoots are manifestly descended from the self-same gorilla, or kangaroo, or Norway rat, whichever animal-Adam the Darwinians trace them to."

—Mark Twain, *Roughing It*

R ▲ ▲ ▲ ▲ ▲ ▲ ▲ ▲ ▲ ▲ ▲ ▲ ▲ ▲ ▲ ▲ ▲ ▲ ▲
UFUS SUNDAYMAN volunteered to take me
on a turkey shoot. We hiked the better part of a day trying
to find a flock of turkeys by their tracks. Around dusk we
came upon a flock just as they were settling into their
roosting tree. That tree looked like it had big brown balls
of mistletoe in it, the flock numbered about thirty or forty.
Content with having all the turkeys in the tree, Rufus said,
"What we do now, doc, is we go camp somewhere and get
up before dawn. Then we come back here and shoot as
many goddamn birds as we can." It was a cold night, and
we slept well. We got up at daybreak, went back to the
tree, and all the turkeys were gone. Rufus said, "They must
have left just minutes before." So we spent the second day

tracking again. Toward the late afternoon we finally came upon our flock, and we each shot a single turkey. Walking back to camp, Rufus happened to spot a bobcat. He shot it. A beautiful little animal with long fur. Rufus was determined to stuff it, but he had no money, and he wondered how he could store it until he did have the money. I said it was no problem. I had that large double-size government freezer in my garage. So we stuffed the bobcat into a big plastic bag and plunked it down on top of my ducks and my hindquarter of deer. It stayed there for months. I got rather used to the hideous snarl on its face and just pushed it aside when I'd reach in for a frozen steak.

The garage was full of black-widow spiders, common in the Southwest, and I was afraid to try to work on anything in there. I hate spiders. They scare the hell out of me even when they're not poisonous. The overhead door was stuck at a height of five feet, and one morning I forgot to duck, hit it, and broke my nose. I got to work late. My nose looked only mildly deformed, but I was getting black-and-blue under the eyes. When I passed Max Rubenstein in the hall, I said, "Hey, I think I broke my nose." Max looked at me and said, "By golly, you're right." I said, "What do I do about it?" Before I knew what was happening, Max reached over and grabbed the thing and shoved it back into line. It was so quick I hardly knew what hit me, and I had tears rolling down my face. But my nose looked really straight now, better than before I broke it. Later I reflected on the way Max had done it, just like that, no self-doubt, no tentativeness. I guess physicians tend to have a bit of a God complex. But it is probably necessary. If I have a colleague working on me, I want him to have a big ego.

That night around 1:00 A.M. Gordon James ended up
in the clinic after he was pretty badly roughed up by the
cops when they threw him in jail. They had billy-clubbed
him on the head, and he had a bad gash up top. He was
also in about stage-three coma from inebriation—just working around his head was giving me a high. I suppose that
might explain my bravado in what procedure to follow. I
shaved Gordon's head—the cut was about two inches long
and gaping—and I draped it up very carefully so that it
would be sterile. I put some local novocaine in it and put
towel clips around the drapes. Towel clips are evil little
pincers with points on them that pierce the skin and hold
the drapes close to the skull so that the field is kept sterile.
I gently cleaned out the wound, and much to my dismay
there were several bone fragments. I could actually see the
covering of the brain, the dura mater. It looked pretty intact.
I put an extra drape over his skull and took him back to
X-ray and got an excellent picture of Gordon James's skull.
Yes, he had a depressed fracture right in the center of his
head. Since the dura wasn't torn, it looked like it would
be a pretty routine matter simply to uplift the bone a little
bit and push the fragments around. That way I'd save myself
an ambulance trip to Roswell or El Paso.

I asked Max Rubenstein to come give me a hand. We
were elaborately set up, and beginning to do this job, things
were going smoothly, we were mentally patting ourselves
on the back for doing pretty good primitive neurosurgery,
and then all at once Gordon sat bolt upright and tore all
the towel clips out, along with little pieces of scalp. He
looked me in the eye and said, "Doc, what can I do to help
ya?" I said, "You just did it, Gordon." We had him lie
back down, and got him into the ambulance and took him

down to the neurosurgeon in El Paso. My ambulance driver was Woodrow Wilson, sober, so I only had to sit in the back and make sure Gordon didn't try to help us any more.

I guess, all things considered, I must have worked longer and harder at Mescalero than I had at any time before or since. I was on call virtually around the clock and never knew what was coming in next. An old woman had what she thought was cancer on her leg. When she finally came in for help, she brought along with her the worst odor you could imagine. She was wearing big heavy winter socks; when I took a pair of scissors to trim off the socks, I found the leg teeming with maggots, cupful after cupful of little white squirming worms. I put a garbage bag around the foot and went to work. The worms had done a damn good job in eating away all the rotten flesh, and it looked like a mummy's leg, skin all shriveled down in among the tendons; meat would appear, and then disappear, and then appear again in another place. It made me rather sick, and I was still queasy when I went on to treat an old Apache lady, Charlotte Pena, a devout Catholic, who had almost completely destroyed her liver. She had had problems with excessive vaginal bleeding, and because of her liver disease she had low platelets and wouldn't clot properly. She was very near death. I did everything I could think of, with fresh frozen plasma and clotting factors; I knew that our best hope would be to send her to intensive care in El Paso. I called ahead, and the chief resident down there said it sounded to him like a gynecological problem, she didn't belong in his unit. I said, "For Christ's sake, she's bleeding to death, she needs your unit, your clotting factors, *and* a gynecologist." He said, "She's an old cirrhotic Indian and I can't help you," and hung up.

I was so mad I couldn't see straight. I sat fuming in my office. I was furious with that sonofabitch resident in El Paso, and I was furious because it didn't matter whether Charlotte stayed here or went there, either way I knew she would surely die. I hate it when I can't do anything.

"You don't look so hot."

I turned, and there was Annie standing in my doorway.

"No," I said, "I probably don't."

"You're angry. And you're tired."

I hadn't noticed that I was tired. But now I did, she was right, I was exhausted.

Annie whispered, "Charlotte's not going to make it, is she?"

I shook my head.

Annie waited, and we looked at each other for a moment. Then she went back down the hall. I found her a few minutes later, with Charlotte, holding her hand. I stood there watching them. Charlotte was very brave and a little talkative, telling Annie stories about her grandkids. In a pool of low lamplight, holding hands, two Indian ladies— I felt like an intruder.

At last Annie said to her, "Do you want me to call anyone in your family, so they can know where you are and what's happening?"

Charlotte didn't respond, she was fading in and out.

Eventually Annie added, "Do you want to say anything to anyone? Maybe you'd like to see a priest." Charlotte nodded her head. Annie turned and looked at me; I went back to my office and called a Catholic father to come give Charlotte Pena the last rites.

Which, I decided later, maybe I should not have done. It outraged some of the family members, especially one of

Charlotte's grandsons, who said that I had destroyed her will to live, she lost her fighting spirit when that priest gave her the last rites. I didn't say anything, just looked at the floor and let him talk.

Annie was especially good with teenagers. One girl had come in with a bacterial infection, open lesions on her vagina; she had been given medicine and sent home. But several hours later she was brought back in crying with pain. She had to go to the bathroom, she desperately had to go, but she wouldn't allow herself to because of the pain of the urine on the open lesions. Annie took the girl into a bathroom, but she couldn't get the kid to uncross her legs. Annie said to her, "I can't put a tube in, this is not the answer." And then, after much talk, Annie got the girl's legs uncrossed, poured cold water over the pubic area, and the girl finally peed. Peed eternally. The cold water really did nothing, the girl just believed that it did.

Annie was real good at making kids believe they could do things they didn't think they could do. With another girl, an obese girl who had tried to OD on drugs, Annie had to insert a stomach tube, and instill activated charcoal and sorbitol to absorb and flush out any poison left in there. Teenagers are not inclined to be terribly cooperative anyway, and with this girl Annie took a very firm, no-nonsense approach: "If you want to fight me and pull this tube out, that's fine. But this tube is going in, regardless of what you do. I'll be careful, and I'll do it as gently as I can, and I'll tell you what I'm doing, and I will ask you to help me, and we'll do it with as little uproar as possible. But, believe me, the tube will go in." And it did. In went the activated charcoal, black as could be, mixed with a dose of sorbitol, which causes extreme diarrhea. It was put down the tube, and it didn't sit too well on the stomach. A lot of the stuff got heaved back up, and Annie came out looking like a spotted leopard. The stuff smears when you try to mop it up, and Annie had it in her hair, on her face, all over her white uniform. I caught a look at her in a lavatory: covered with the gunk, she was just staring at herself in the mirror.

There was so much sorrow, despair, and hopelessness among the teenagers. Young Indians took their lives without any true concept of the finality of what they were doing. They thought of the pain they wanted some other person to feel, but somehow it didn't strike home that they were truly ending the only life they had. In a world of ranching and farming, kids growing up to be cowboys, always around lariats and ropes, a main method was hanging. The family would find their pride and joy hanging in the barn. In the ER you could see the engorgement and the marks of the rope. You could see the marks on them when they were lain in the casket. The undertakers didn't waste much time on cosmetology, the bodies were just popped into town, embalmed, and then sent back to the reservation, where the men washed up the male bodies and the women washed up the female bodies. Annie was a real comfort to the families, helping them to pick out burial clothes, sticking close to them; she'd give them the towels and washcloths and shampoo. Sometimes the rope burns were covered with just a piece of wrapping paper.

▲ ▲ ▲ ▲ ▲ ▲ ▲ ▲ ▲ ▲ ▲ ▲ ▲ ▲ ▲ ▲ ▲ ▲ ▲ ▲

I N L A T E S E P T E M B E R, Annie invited Max and me to join her and Silas for dinner. She told me how to get there, her house was ten miles away, high on a little summit. Navigating the winding dirt road up to it, I wondered how she made it home during the heavy winter snow. When I reached the top I saw a small whitewashed frame house that had been added on to (later that night she told me the carpenters had been students of hers at Tularosa High). Annie Messenger Bird Lester Mendez didn't seem to care much for material things, but she clearly had put a lot of time and work into the place. Flanking the front door were two big old whiskey barrels filled with zinnias, petunias, geraniums. When nobody answered my knock I just went inside. There were books everywhere, filling the shelves from floor to ceiling. The furniture was simple and old, and she had distributed big floor pillows in soft colors. Some pretty amazing Indian pottery. Only one houseplant, a huge jade, by the west windows.

But where was she? Tentatively I called her name. No answer. I put down my bottle of wine among the clutter of the kitchen and walked out onto the deck. Then I saw her—she was down by a big pond fussing with a barbecue, her hair in a long black braid. I walked down to join her, and she gave me a wonderful smile and then a soft kiss, on the mouth.

"How," I said, "can I not even *think* about it?"

"Not even think about what?"

"Right." There was a vegetable garden with neat little rows of beans, peas, tomatoes, and cucumbers.

Annie, though, had the big picture in mind; with her barbecue fork she pointed out at the green hills and the vastness of the twilight sky. "Like it?"

"Very much."

We walked back up to the house, where I opened the bottle of wine I'd brought. We sat sipping out on the deck. I asked her if her students at Tularosa High School were any good, and she said that most all of the kids would stay close to home—they had severely limited, localized aspirations. The girls kept getting pregnant. Teacher's pet, Michael, football star and honor student, probably wouldn't go to college. "Mike," she sighed, "is so smart, doesn't drink at all. On Friday nights this whole area turns out for the games. And Michael's parents, both of them, get falling down drunk by halftime. And I mean *falling down*. It's a terrible humiliation for Mike. I saw him trying to guide his mother to the car, and a big white cop said to him, 'Need some help, chief?' You should have seen the look Mike gave him."

I nodded.

We heard the *vroom-vroom* of a motorcycle pulling into the driveway. It was Silas, Annie's darling boy. He wore little granny glasses, and his long black hair in a ponytail. He was sixteen or seventeen, and he gave me one of those limp Indian handshakes, helped himself to a glass of wine, and seated himself firmly on the deck. He was a volunteer teacher's aide in the Head Start program, and he told us about Ellen, a little retarded girl who at recess always hung upside down from a tree limb and who today had invented a story that ended with her saying, "They smashed us into *mustard!*"

Annie went inside and returned with a platter of steak fillets.

Silas held out to me a marijuana cigarette, and I wanted to be sociable, but I'd tried marijuana in college, and it had literally burned my lungs, causing a coughing fit that lasted an hour; it had done absolutely nothing for me except make me miserable. I didn't want to do that again. So I passed the grass back to Silas, who promptly passed it on to his mother. I was already about as mellow as need be.

We heard a car. Max Rubenstein. He slouched in, wearing a Boston Red Sox baseball cap over his flowing red hair and a big "Marxist-Leninist T-shirt," which had pictures on the back of Groucho and John. He had brought along a couple of cartons of ice cream, which he put in the fridge before coming out onto the deck to join us. He said urgently, a little flustered, "Quick, somebody help me. I must unburden myself of a joke—I have been aching to tell it."

Annie grinned and said, "Unburden thyself."

"No, I can't, I hate jokes." He sat down huddled into himself, the way tall guys sometimes do, as if trying to make themselves smaller. When Annie passed him the joint Max took a drag that would have stunned a horse. Holding it all in, he said in a high squeaky voice, "So why don't you want to hear my joke?"

The inane byplay continued a little, and finally, after a second enormous toke, Max looked at us and said, "Well, a man went into an insane asylum. In the first room he found a guy doing this—" Max threw a phantom ball in the air and hit it with a phantom bat. "And our visitor asked him, 'What are you going to do when you get out of here?' The guy said, 'I'm going to be a big-league baseball player.' "

Silas and Annie and I were smiling, all three of us waiting.

"He goes into the second room, where he finds a guy doing this—" and here Max lavishly imitated playing the violin. "The man says, 'What are you going to do when you get out of here?' The guy says, 'I'm going to play in a symphony orchestra.' Our visitor goes into a third room, and he finds a guy standing there naked with his dick in a big jar of Planters Peanuts. Our visitor says, 'What are you going to do when you get out of here?' and the guy says, 'Get out of here? I'll never get out of here—can't you see I'm *fucking nuts?*' "

We all three laughed, especially Annie. And Max looked about five years old, terribly proud of himself, like a little boy after his first piano recital.

We sat there awhile, gossiping and admiring the view. Annie and Max did most of the talking, about someone I didn't know, but it was more fun that way—I concentrated on Annie and Max, the way they said things to each other and listened to each other, the intimacy between them. They both seemed to admire very much the person they were talking about. Then Annie gave us our tasks to perform—Silas to grill the steaks, me to set the big picnic table, Max to help her carry stuff out from the kitchen.

It was a wonderful dinner. I had two big bowls of the cold cucumber soup, and I think I said at least twice, "This is dee-licious." I felt the same way about the steak and baked potato and fresh peas. The sunset was extraordinary, the afterglow turning the whole endless sky into a cool mauve.

For dessert Annie had baked an apple pie. We all had big slices, à la mode with Max's ice cream, and our talk wandered back to Annie's classes at Tularosa High. She shook her head. "Years ago, when I substituted in second grade, the kids were so warm and open and affectionate. When we're on the reservation, when everybody's an Indian—you know? It's only when we get older and have to live in the white man's world that we—"

"Mom," Silas said, "give it a rest."

She looked a little hurt and said, "I know I go on too much. Probably because I'm so used to *teaching*. But at least I'm not like the chair of our English department, Miss Gordon—she asks the kids who they'd rather have as a friend, Emerson or Hawthorne. 'Who would you rather room with, Wordsworth or Coleridge?'"

"Coleridge, of course," Max said. "He's got all the drugs."

———

Annie went into the house and came back with two large candelabra. Silas lighted all the candles, and we sat in their glow and the surrounding, deepening darkness. I felt a little out of it, since the other three were quite stoned. At one point Max rose to the bait of Annie's needling, and he said in a wildly confidential tone to me, "Ms. Messenger Bird, left to her own devices, can be suspicious, possessive, too mawkish by half, constantly hyperventilating her sentimental outrage—" And then Max looked at me more carefully, with those crazy green eyes, and said, "But she is essentially a pushover."

Annie kicked him.

Silas went down to the pond. Max said he had some work to do. We said good-bye, and then Annie and I were alone on the candlelit deck. I said, "It's very pleasant to watch you and Max talk."

"Oh, he's my sweetheart."

I was suddenly crushed. "He is?"

She looked up at me. "Well, no—"

"You make a lovely couple."

She was still looking at me. "Gosh, Jimmy, don't you—uh—don't you—?" She leaned toward me and said, in the slow, overly emphatic way one speaks to a deaf person, "Max plays on the other team."

"Oh," I replied. And then, as it sank in, I said it again: "*Oh*."

"I love to dance with Max, he is absolutely the best dancer in the world. But that's as far as we go, kid."

Kid?

"I *told* you. That morning after I disgraced myself at your house. After you plied me with liquor—"

"You did? I did what?"

"Don't you remember? In the morning, when I had that splitting headache? God, I was ragged. And I told—"

I was trying to remember. And then I did remember, I visualized it, she was at the door— "Oh, I thought you meant Loretta—"

"Lor*etta?*"

Loretta was our public health nurse, she'd been a WAVE, and she was extremely formidable (I was scared of her); Loretta was all business. I had dropped in on her immunization clinics and her well-baby clinics, and one day we went out on her rounds to remote parts of the reservation. The poor kids, stuff pouring out of their ears, flies clustered in the corners of their eyes. Loretta would dispense ointment. We couldn't get clean water to bathe the wounds. Loretta marched right in and did the best job she could, a career public health officer in her khaki uniform and navy hat. "She's so masculine. I thought she was—I guess—"

"Jimmy, don't you know who people *are?*"

"No. No, I guess I don't." I was visualizing Max, his hallucinatory green eyes. "So, Max is a—"

"Homosexual. Go ahead, Jim, you can do it. Max Rubenstein is a dear and glorious physician, but he has no interest in me as a lover. He *may* have some interest in Silas."

I visualized that. As best I could. I said, "Where has that boy gone to now?"

"Down to the pond."

"Oh, right. Silas went there."

"Yes, Silas *went* there. Jesus, Jimmy, I get shit faced at your house, and you get moronic at mine."

"We're made for each other." I said it, and concentrated: Loretta is not a lesbian. Max is a homosexual. That's the way it is. They never tell you anything in the service.

Annie had a cigarette. So did I. I didn't know what to do with it, since I don't smoke. I said, "How come your last name is Mendez?"

"Oh, I just married Vittorio so he wouldn't get drafted." Vittorio?

"We never even slept together. It was just something I did to help."

"And your first husband? He's the one—he's the son of Barnabas Lester, and he is the father of the Silas Lester who is at the *pond*—"

"You are making giant strides, darling."

"And where is *he*? The father of Silas?"

"Who knows?"

"That's too bad."

"Yes. Last we heard he was a police officer somewhere in Texas."

I stared at her in the candlelight. I said, "Does Silas get along with his Grandfather Lester?"

Annie tilted her head sideways. "My esteemed father-in-law is a real piece of work. You ought to see him in a courtroom. He eats those BIA lawyers for breakfast. And he can turn corners you don't even know are there. Down the hill"—she waved her hand at the darkness in the valley—"that Olympic-size swimming pool he's so proud of. He got it on a request for 'hydrotherapy for otherwise unemployable males.'" She laughed. "Oh, Barnabas Lester is *something*."

"I see," I said, though I didn't really see. Or what in

fact I saw was Annie's son, Silas, coming slowly back up the hill. When he reached the deck his mother said, "Honey, play us something. Where's your guitar?"

He said, "I'm wasted." He wandered into the house. "Good-night, Ma. Good-night, Jim."

After a bit she stood up and told me she wanted me to come listen to something. I followed her into the living room. I sat on a big white ottoman while she strolled over and put something into the tape deck. Then I heard the most amazing piece of popular music—I don't know, it wasn't like the Beatles, who always made me feel happy, and it wasn't like The Doors, who always made me feel a little nervous and edgy. Whatever it was, it was really something. I said, "Who are those guys?"

"Silas."

"But there're at least three voices, and a bass and drums and—"

"You can do that now, Jimmy. In a studio."

"All those voices and instruments are Silas?"

"Yep."

I didn't quite follow the "story" the first time around, but it seemed to be an old Indian legend transposed to rock 'n' roll. All of Silas's voices were singing:

The grass was young and I was horseback,

The warriors sang a sacred song,
The thunder was like drumming,

All over the sky a voice was calling,

A voice from a secret place
Where the universe was born—

All along, all through it, ran a refrain, "Messenger Bird, Messenger Bird." When the song was done I sprang up from my ottoman and said, "Oh, please, please let me hear that again."

Annie smiled, went over, and punched the machine. I stared past her out the window at the candles still flickering on the deck. I went out and got them and brought them in. I turned off the lights. We heard that remarkable song again, "Messenger Bird," in the soft glow. I could not help it, I took Annie's hand and turned her to me, a little like an invitation to dance, but then I stopped her and held her and searched her eyes.

She was frightened. She stiffened. "Don't, Jim. For almost four years now—I've lived without it. I get lonely, but I don't get crazy. My life is fine, thank you. I don't *need* that."

I whispered, "Sure you do . . ."

A ▲
T FIVE O'CLOCK one morning I answered
the night bell at the hospital to find a man with a baby in
his arms. The man said, "I think my baby's dead." So I
took the baby from him, and I looked at it, and it was cold,
and it was blue. There was nothing to be done, the man
was right, it was dead. The man said he was afraid he could
not claim it as his own because he and its mother weren't
married. The mother had gone off somewhere out of state.
Oklahoma, maybe. The man claimed he had awakened at
four o'clock to feed the baby and had found it this way. I
was suspicious, something about his story didn't ring right.
At seven I called Barnabas Lester, and Barnabas called the
tribal police. They came and talked to the man. After they

left, the man just sat there holding the baby. He wouldn't give it back to me. I argued a little, to no avail, and so I called Barnabas again. This time he came down himself. They talked, and on my way out, to leave them alone together, I happened to glance back. The man was weeping, and Barnabas took the baby out of his arms. Barnabas patted the dead baby and talked to it and rocked it. I thought to myself that I wouldn't have expected Barnabas Lester to do that, and then I forgot about it.

A code was called in the emergency room around eleven o'clock in the morning. A little three-year-old girl had been standing with her parents right outside the general store, the parents turned their backs on her for a moment, talking to another couple, and the girl wandered off, out into the parking lot, just as a big full-sized Chevy truck with a large rear bumper backed out of a slot, and the truck hit the kid perfectly on the forehead, caved in her skull right there, the nose and forehead were just ruined, and the parents had whipped the girl into their car and rushed her up here. The heart was still beating, but the facial bones were all crushed inward; there was a little hole about the size of a quarter through which you could see the brain. She was all mangled and mashed, we did the little things we could do, but the kid was demolished. She died. In a very short time, a lot of neighbors and relatives showed up, as if by magic (since so few people had telephones), and there was terrible wailing in the hospital lobby.

And of course the wards are full of patients who have to be seen. So you clean yourself up, and somebody talks with the little girl's family, and somebody else does the paperwork, and the rest of us go back to walking into patients' rooms and saying, "Hi, how are you doing today?" You go to the clinic, you take care of colds and runny noses.

It bugged me that the Indians didn't seem capable of directly answering my questions. If I asked, "When did this problem start?" the Indian would tell me his life story. They'd talk around a subject, not directly about it. And I guess doctors did come across to them as impatient—and uncaring. For instance, I spent way too much time with one old guy who had a backache. I wanted to know where it hurt and when it started. But his answers took me through every major battle of World War II. He sat there saying he had a terrible, terrible pain, and I said, "Where is it?"

"Well, in Iwo Jima . . ."

"Is it in your back?"

"Yes."

"Below the belt line?"

"Yes."

"Does it hurt when you breathe?"

"No, but on Okinawa . . ."

By the time I finished with him I had a dozen patients backed up. You go through the waiting room crowded with expressionless, silent Indians, the noise of the "Flintstones" blaring from the TV, and you find sitting there, in the consulting room, a four-foot-ten Apache woman who weighs two hundred pounds and has a blood sugar of over four hundred. And you know she has tried three times to OD, she's heard voices telling her to. She says she lives alone, but then you find out that she lives with her husband and nine-year old daughter. The daughter is "in first grade again." So you help the Apache woman to her feet, and she's angry. You have made her promise that she will stop huffing gas and stop going to "Lysol houses," where the mixture of disinfectant or hair spray with orange soda really turns the trick.

Sometimes the job gets you so discouraged that you are angry for days at a time. One night I was taking care of a tiny infant girl only about a month old who had developed a truly terrible pneumonia. She had gotten progressively sicker and had reached the point where she wasn't able to breathe on her own. Respirators were something that only the larger medical centers had. We certainly did not. I put a tiny tracheostomy in this precious infant and was able to act as a human respirator by giving her little puffs of air. I then decided Roswell would be the place to send her, since Roswell did have respirators for infants. None of the nurses nor anybody else in the hospital was willing to go get Rufus Sundayman to tell him he had to drive the ambulance that night. So I left Pita breathing for the baby and drove over to Rufus's house and with considerable dread opened the gate in the fence. The reason nobody would approach him was the three or four vicious dogs he kept within that fence. I was immediately surrounded by them and their snarling, but those dogs were more bark than bite, and I found Rufus in his usual euphoric state of moderate inebriation. I drove him back to the hospital, and we quickly hopped into the ambulance. I got in the back with the infant girl and played human respirator for the hour and a half that it took to get over to Roswell. It was exhausting, and I really couldn't worry about Rufus's driving because I had to pay strict attention not to breathe too hard and overextend the baby's lungs. When we arrived in the outskirts of Roswell I could see the glow of city lights in the night sky, and I thought, "Thank God, we will be there shortly," and within a few minutes more we had come to a halt. But nothing was happening. I peeked over the back of the front seat and said, "Rufus, why aren't they helping us get the baby out of the ambulance?" Rufus said, "I don't know, but I don't think I'm at the hospital." I looked around. We were in a lovers' lane, with our little Public Health Service ambulance surrounded by convertibles and passionate teenagers. "Rufus, for Christ's sake, you've been to Roswell about a hundred times. Why aren't you at the hospital?" Rufus said, "Well, I just got a little confused. I really don't know what part of town I'm in." I went back to breathing for the baby, and it took Rufus forty-five minutes more to find his way to the hospital. The baby was in extremis, I was in extremis, and Rufus was in dire danger of a doctor-induced homicide. We finally got the baby into the hospital and on a respirator. But she died in spite of everything that could be done. On the way back to Mescalero, I drove, and I really let Rufus have it. Although nothing, probably, could have saved her. Rufus didn't say a word.

I think that was the all-time worst week of my first year at the hospital. I also had a big forty-two-year-old Apache man whom I'd just admitted with a heart attack. We had lidocaine and a monitor to keep track of the heartbeat. Barnabas had recently acquired a DC cardioverter for us, which is the device you apply to the chest when the patient develops a lethal heart rhythm. The representative of the company who delivered it had told me it was "foolproof." That night my patient got into trouble; he went into ventricular tachycardia with a pulse of 180 and very low blood pressure. I hooked him up, followed the directions the way I'd been told to, put the paddles on, pushed the button, and *bam!* he died on the spot.

A ▲ ▲ ▲ ▲ ▲ ▲ ▲ ▲ ▲ ▲ ▲ ▲ ▲ ▲ ▲ ▲ ▲ ▲ ▲
L M O S T   E V E R Y   F A M I L Y   on the reservation
seemed to have lost a child before it reached maturity—
from a car wreck, alcohol abuse, suicide, a fight, a knife or
gunshot wound. I could read in the mothers' eyes the knowledge that one or more of their children wouldn't live to see
twenty-one.

In the ER, if you'd ask a woman how she got that
broken nose, you'd get two kinds of answers—obviously
false ("Oh, I fell down the stairs") or obviously true ("Oh,
my husband was displeased with me"). Over in the south-
eastern corner of the reservation was a little community—
more like a club, really—called White City (because, I
think, the half-dozen shacks were all whitewashed). The

thugs who lived there often went on violent rampages: they'd drink, sniff glue or an especially popular gold-colored spray paint, and then get on their horses and tear around the reservation attacking people. They'd see an elderly woman sitting on her porch, ride by, and whack her with a four-by-four. No rhyme or reason. They'd smash a little kid's head with a pipe. Whenever these bastards would go crazy we'd suddenly have eight or ten badly injured people to deal with. A real bloodbath. Meanwhile, the White City gang would ride their horses up into the hills where the police cars couldn't follow.

One night in the ER I had already treated a teenager who had drunk Clorox. I also had a two-year-old girl who had fallen (or was pushed) into a campfire, and she was badly injured from the coals; she'd probably lose an eye, an eye that I had to irrigate immediately. While I was doing that, the child screaming in pain, a cop brought in a girl who had fallen off a horse and probably ruptured a lung. I had those three kids to worry about when the victims of another White City raid started to limp in.

You really have no warning about what's coming through the door, and frequently you are not dealing with someone you can reason with. If an aggrieved patient is intent on retaliation for some real or imagined harm, he'll find out where you live and come to your house. Annie was extremely patient with these town drunks and seemed genuinely to understand them. They usually had families who formed a protective care system, but a few guys were so far gone that their families had given up on them. Bernard Rideout was a great athlete gone to ruin; now in his mid-thirties, he'd drink, huff Lysol, and end up broke and crazy; like many other guys in his situation, he'd eventually wander up to Annie's house, where he knew he could count on a hot meal, some of Silas's cast-off clothes, and a place to sleep until he was capable of getting himself over to detox.

One night Annie and Silas stayed late in Tularosa for a social function, and I was alone at their house waiting for them to return. Around nine-thirty I answered a loud banging at the door to discover Bernard standing there totally bombed. He wanted to see Annie, and he leered at me as if their appointment was sexual. I told Bernard that Annie wasn't there, watched him slink away, and went back to my *New England Journal of Medicine.* Twenty minutes later there was an even louder pounding on the door, and now Bernard shouted at me, "I know she's in there! You just hiding her." I tried to reason with him, even invited him in for a cup of strong coffee, but he wandered off into the night again, muttering about "getting some help." That made me nervous. I knew I could handle Bernard all right, but if "help" meant a gun or friends I was in trouble. I sat in the stillness of Annie's living room. I paced about, fussed with the fire, and went into the kitchen, where I poured myself a stiff shot of whiskey. I drank it down and was on my way back to the living room when I jumped a foot— Bernard was out on the deck, a machete in hand, his face pressed grotesquely against the glass door.

I called the cops, who came, poked around the property, found Bernard passed out under a tree, and carted him down to the lockup. I sat by the dying fire, my heart beating. I tried to make fun of myself by remembering how terrified I had been when I was seven years old and saw the movie *The Thing.* Pretty tame by today's standards, but when I was a little boy it scared the bejesus out of me. I couldn't fall asleep at night. I was always seeing the Thing in the Greenhouse, the Thing suddenly *close* (much as I had now seen Bernard on the deck). I'd call for my father to come lie down beside me, but he said I had to grow up and master my childish fears. Mom intervened (she knew what fear was), and Dad told her to go lie down beside her wimpy boy. The wimpy boy, however, knew Mom wasn't *big* enough to protect him from the Thing. I needed Dad. But I heard him yell at my mother, "How do you expect me to make a man out of him?" (And I heard her shout back, "I *don't!*") So, after much grumbling, Dad came in and lay down beside me, making clear to me that in his judgment I was a sissy. I desperately wanted not to be, desperately wanted to please him. On my eighth birthday, after dinner and cake, I told my father that I had something to show him. Dramatically I opened the cellar door and walked down the creaky steps into the pitch-black basement. In the spine-tingling dark I crept over to where the furnace was, behind which I knew the Thing was waiting for me, and I sang up to my father, "I'm not afraid!" No, I was petrified—and I really hurt myself when I banged my head on something in the dark. I ran back upstairs wailing, "Daddy—my head went *boyying!*"

My father loved to tell that story, imitating his Brave Little Scout's voice trilling, *"Boyying!"*

Working with Annie, I sometimes saw her as a kid in a dark basement. Except it wasn't an imaginary Thing that had got to her; it was Mescalero, and the monsters were real. This kid didn't run. Annie couldn't keep fear entirely out of her eyes, or her voice, but she hurled herself into every hardest part of the job. One afternoon a guy with a gun, very drunk and very angry, blundered in and totally destroyed the ER, tore everything apart, ripped up records. It all happened so fast, I guess I was in shock for a minute. Before I was able to start dealing with it, it was over. Somehow Annie managed to wrestle the weapon away from the drunk and hold him at his own gunpoint until help arrived.

I saw her doing all these things, and suddenly I realized I was in love with her. I'd never been in love before. But if Annie could do this sucker, goddamn it, so could Jim. When things got especially hairy in the ER, I'd mutter to myself, *"Boyying"* under my breath.

▲ ▲

N E V E R   R E A L L Y understood what the medicine men did. I was introduced to a couple of them, but they were old and wouldn't talk to me. Annie told me that patients seemed to select themselves out—those who had emotional or psychiatric problems would go to a medicine man, and those who had pneumonia or broken bones or babies to be delivered ended up with Max and me. If an older person came in with an illness we knew we couldn't cure, we'd just quit. We weren't forced by the Public Health Service to keep hopeless cases on I.V.s or in any way prolong their agony; we'd just make them comfortable, give them morphine, and let 'em leave. It was practical, obviously the better part of wisdom. Nowadays death is not an acceptable outcome; we refuse to let nature take its course, and so everybody ends up dying in a hospital, hooked up to machines, instead of at home with loved ones.

There was no veterinarian to serve on the "rez," so I filled in as best I could. Once a horse was brought to me with a big boil the size of an orange on its neck. It was a very fine-looking horse. The proud owner held the horse's head as tightly as he could while I stood on a chair and took a good-sized knife to it. I made a two-inch-deep incision straight through the boil, and all sorts of foul-smelling greenish pus flew out all over me and down the horse's neck. The horse reared, and I dropped the knife, which fell, blade down, right through my loafer, it sank in through the leather and just stood there quivering. It hurt like hell, but I didn't want to make too much of a fuss about it, so I told the owner to hand me the needle I had prepared— the biggest syringe we had—and I gave the horse ten million units of aqueous penicillin. I got down off the chair, away from the horse, and looked at my shoe. There was that damn knife sticking up. I pulled the knife out, and blood immediately pulsed out of the top of my loafer. I stumbled back into the hospital, looked at the foot, and gave myself the strongest antibiotic we had in the drug cabinet, Keflin—I didn't know what kind of germs were all over that knife blade.

A very small puppy was born with all its intestinal tract outside of its abdomen, everything all curled around in a circle and hanging out from the puppy's abdominal wall. Max and I waited until the pup was about four weeks old, and then on my kitchen table we gave him open-drop ether, because we wanted to relax the abdominal muscles. Max opened everything up, loosened all the intestine from the outside, pushed it all to the inside, and tucked everything back in and sewed him up. But the puppy had a cardiac arrest; Max was pumping that teeny little chest with his hand, I was breathing for the pup with a small endotracheal tube that I had slipped down his windpipe, and we spent an hour trying to revive our Skipper. Without success.

Before I was even in medical school I had known I wanted to be a surgeon. I wanted to learn to cut and tie knots and do really complicated work. Whenever I'd play golf, as I walked between shots, I used to do all sorts of intricate knots one-handed on the strap of my bag. But I was afraid that I might not be able to do it. I wasn't sure I could handle emotionally all the blood and gore. The summer of my senior year I went to Ithaca, to the Ag School at Cornell, and took a butchery class. The first time I saw a cow slaughtered, I said to myself I couldn't do it. The cattle came in from a lot right next to the building, through a chute they walked down one by one. A gate would shut behind them so that they couldn't move. You'd take a stun gun, which is essentially just a bolt, and put a .45 cartridge in right behind the bolt, which propels it right through whatever is in front of it for two inches. You grab this thing and hold it over the cow's skull and fire it right into the forehead. And then the cow, this big cow, looks at you, because what you have just done doesn't kill the cow right away, the creature just looks at you, and its eyes say, "Holy *fuck!* What the hell did you just *do* to me?" The cow has this incredibly frightened look on its face, and it lets out a huge sound, a combination of moo and scream, a horrible bellow. All this adrenaline rushes out, along with sweat and shit, as the cow falls down on its knees shaking; one wall of the chute flips the cow down onto a ramp to the killing floor. Then you grab a chain, a regular old link chain like for towing cars, and you quickly wrap it around the cow's back legs and hoist the cow up, you crank it and crank it, and you've got the cow upside down by its hind legs. The cow is still alive and roaring. You take a huge knife and slice its jugular, which is like releasing Niagara Falls, buckets of thick red blood, you get drenched in it, and the cow is *still* alive, bellowing, shaking, and its eyes are saying, "What are you *doing?* I'm still *alive!*" Then this guy, a graduate student in meat cutting who is doing some study on muscles, needs a fresh specimen from the gastroc muscle on the hind leg, and he takes a quick slice, chopping it out all fresh, and the still-living cow has turned to look at him, with this torrent of blood still pouring out of its throat. The smell and the heat, you stagger back, you feel yourself losing your footing . . .

A

▲ ▲ ▲ ▲ ▲ ▲ ▲ ▲ ▲ ▲ ▲ ▲ ▲ ▲ ▲ ▲ ▲ ▲ ▲

POOR APACHE LADY, Wanda Wing, had been cut on the temple with a bottle. The area had gradually ulcerated out until it was a wound about the size of a dime. Wanda had treated it by stuffing a dirty Kleenex in it. About every third day she'd change the dirty Kleenex. Gradually the wound went from the size of a dime to that of a nickel, to a quarter, to a silver dollar. Eventually she came in to the hospital, and she had this horrible deep ulceration going right down to the muscle, over her temple, exuding pus and smelling bad. Wanda still had her Kleenexes in there, several of them wadded in. I cleaned the wound out as best I could, cut away all the dead tissue, and gave her the most potent antibiotic we had. I kept her in the hospital, where I soaked the wound three or four times a day. Within a week it was a nice, clean silver dollar. But it was quite clear that she was going to be left with a large ugly scar. I didn't have the vaguest idea how to do a skin graft. Max was off for the week. So I put a fairly long slit in the scalp underneath her hair, which I had shaved off, to loosen up all the tissue of the scalp down to the silver dollar. I was able to pull the upper edges of the wound down to the lower edges and suture them together. That made a small half-moon linear scar on her temple. With a little more tugging and pulling, I was able to get it all together, and, lo and behold, when I looked at it three weeks later I was so proud of myself. A scar, but certainly not a disfiguring scar. You couldn't see a thing underneath where the hair was growing back in. My first and only attempt at plastic surgery. Pretty cute.

But when you practice medicine on an Indian reservation you don't have much time to congratulate yourself. So much of that work involves failure. I was treating one seventy-year-old man, Bob Blaylock, a cancer patient, with whom I had long talks late at night when everyone was asleep. He told me about the Indian schools of his youth. Really terrible stuff, lye soap baths in vats filled with whimpering boys, punishing doses of castor oil that could buckle your knees, public strappings that went on until the child cried out in pain and shame, violating the Indian tradition of stoicism. The kids were often sent to schools hundreds of miles away and didn't get to see their parents for years. Five generations of kids uprooted from their culture and sent to faraway institutions had led to alcoholism, drug abuse, high unemployment, high divorce rates. Most people have no idea of the abuse that took place in those Indian schools, it was a child-abuse program funded by the federal government and administered by the Bureau of Indian Affairs. Kids were stolen away from their parents at gunpoint. If the parents didn't give up their children, the federal agents said they couldn't have food rations. The sanitation at the schools was rudimentary, tuberculosis rampant, kids whipped for speaking their tribal language. In the 1930s, twenty-four thousand Indian children—one out of three— were rounded up and sent to these boarding schools.

Bob Blaylock was a burly old Apache, broad shouldered, and underneath one of his lungs a lot of water was pushing the lung up, which was why he was gasping for breath and couldn't sleep. I took out of him a liter and a half of yellow watery stuff, and he was immensely relieved. I injected tetracycline in between the layer of lung and the chest wall; you burn the area, you use something caustic. It hurts like hell. I did a biopsy, and clearly Bob had a bad cancer of the type associated with asbestos. He'd changed brake shoes as a mechanic in the army. I had to tell Bob he was going to die. (And he went really quickly, in just about three weeks.) One thing that was nice was that he seemed to sympathize with me and felt bad he was putting *me* through this. So we helped each other. When Bob had first come in, he had said he had a bad cold, but later I was to discover that he knew all along. Before he had come in, he had gone up to Ruidoso and transferred the title of his car to his wife's name. He had taken care of all his affairs; he knew perfectly well he was terminal. And then one morning I went in to see him around 7:00 A.M., I was listening to his chest through my stethoscope, he was asleep, and I heard him just fade away. He was actually dead, the body was giving its last few gasps, reflexively. He had died right there, and I had just happened to walk in on him.

That afternoon I had another ambulance ride down to El Paso with Rufus, who was sober for once. In the hospital down there I wanted to say one more good-bye to Bob Blaylock, whose body had already been transported down. His family wanted an autopsy; they knew they could get money from the government because he had a mesothelioma (an asbestos-related cancer). I went downstairs into the autopsy room, and there he was: on the cold slab of marble with the gutter running around to the drain spouts. The docs took a scalpel, did a quick slice around the face, and before I knew it they were peeling off Bob Blaylock's face, separating skin from bone, at the jaw and then up at the nose, the eyes, and they took his whole face off over his head, and then they took a gizmo and sawed a ring around his head and pulled the top of his skull off like a little cap. Bob Blaylock, a survivor of the BIA school system, sweet old guy . . .

You get used to it. And you do not get used to it. Sometimes you displace it, you feel it a patient later. Stored-up emotions can come out when you least expect them, when you have dropped your guard. It can happen immediately, the emotion takes you over and blows you apart before you even know what has happened. Josie Gaseoma was pregnant with twins, a prime candidate for premature delivery. I put her on strict bed rest, strict pelvic rest, and I explained to her what that meant. A few nights later she was brought into the ER, and her boyfriend—the putative father of the twins—had broken Josie's leg with a baseball bat. "Pelvic rest" insulted his manhood. Pita told me the sonofabitch was still out in the parking lot, and I ran out, and there he was, pacing like a drugged sentry, still carrying the baseball bat. I was dressed in my hospital scrubs, blue bottoms and tops. I walked up to him and shouted, "What the hell are you doing here? You want to break her other leg? Goddamnit, you useless coward, get your ass out of my parking lot!" He gave me an extremely menacing stare, but he got into a car and drove away. When I turned around, shaking with anger, I saw Max Rubenstein standing at the emergency entrance. Max had watched it all, and when I stalked back past him he said, "You some kind of rene-gade cowboy? You crazy?" Eventually I cooled down and thought about it. Of course. Of course I was crazy. The image of a calm, patient physician is frequently that, just an image. By definition, the work you do calls up very basic, turbulent emotions; you say you can handle it, and most of the time you do. At other times, the whole world seems suddenly to shatter into pieces, and you hardly know who you are.

"THE INDIANS that I have had an opportunity of seeing in real life are quite different from those described in poetry. They are by no means the stoics that they are represented; taciturn, unbending, without a tear or a smile. Taciturn they are, it is true, when in company with white men, whose good-will they distrust, and whose language they do not understand; but the white man is equally taciturn under like circumstances. When the Indians are among themselves, however, there cannot be greater gossips. Half their time is taken up in talking over their adventures in war and hunting, and in telling whimsical stories. They are great mimics and buffoons, also, and entertain themselves excessively at the expense of the whites with whom they have associated, and who have supposed them impressed with profound respect for their grandeur and dignity. They are curious observers, noting everything in silence, but with a keen and watchful eye; occasionally exchanging a glance or a grunt with each other, when anything particularly strikes them; but reserving all comments until they are alone. Then it is that they give full scope to criticism, satire, mimicry, and mirth."

—Washington Irving, *Crayon Miscellany*

A

▲ ▲ ▲ ▲ ▲ ▲ ▲ ▲ ▲ ▲ ▲ ▲ ▲ ▲ ▲ ▲ ▲ ▲ ▲ ▲

T THANKSGIVING I was able to get five days off. Annie and I took a little vacation in Mexico. We ran into our first patch of trouble in a small town in Arizona. A cop stopped me, for no reason at all, and wrote me up, he said all I had to do was pay fifty dollars and I could be on my way again.

I was steamed. When I got to the police station I said to this fat clown of a chief, "I'm not going to pay you fifty dollars. I didn't do anything wrong."

The asshole got up from behind his desk, came over to me, put his fist under my chin, and said, "One more word out of you and you'll spend tonight in jail."

I could imagine that and promptly shut up. When I got

the courage to speak again, I said, "I don't have any money, there's no way I can pay you the fifty bucks."

"The bank is open," he said. "Go down to it and get some money."

I had about two hundred dollars in my wallet, but I walked down the street, and I asked this senior officer in the bank why in the world I was being treated so badly.

He said, "Well, that's the way our policemen are. He's doing a good job."

I got my fifty bucks as a bank draft and walked back to the police station. I was really pissed by the time I got there, and I said to the chief that I was going to the justice of the peace.

He told me where to go. On the way, the senior bank officer, going for lunch, spied me and came up to me and said, "So you've met our police chief. You're from New York, aren't you?"

I said I was from New York State but not the city. I was from Syracuse, upstate.

He said, "You're a doctor?"

"Yes."

He said, "Well, goddamn, why didn't you tell us you were from upstate New York instead of New York City? We wouldn't have had to go through all this." He said, "Let me go get your fifty dollars back. You didn't argue with the chief, did you?"

"Yes," I said, "I kind of did."

"Well," he said, "forget about your fifty dollars. But I'll tell you what we'll do, we'll set you up in a clinic here, and we'll pay you a hundred thousand dollars a year, we really need a good doctor. We hate New York City, but the rest of New York State is okay."

"Where is the justice of the peace?"

"Well, you can talk to him, he lives in that little yellow house two blocks up that way, see it? But I don't know as you are going to get too much out of him."

So I went up the street two blocks to that little yellow house. The justice of the peace was about ninety-five years old, he came to the door five minutes after I had rung the bell. Holy Christ, I thought he was going to drop dead right in front of me. "Oh, yeah," he said. "Oh, yeah, our police chief don't like easterners. He gives 'em all tickets, oh, yeah, that's the right thing, our town needs the money."

I said, "Do you feel all right?"

He said, "Oh, yeah, I'm okay."

I said, "Let me help you back into your house." I took him by the elbow and eased him back in, and I helped him down onto his couch.

"Oh, yeah, I'm fine," he said.

I picked up Annie, who had been having a fine time in the malt shop, jawing with a mother-to-be.

Driving along to Mexico, I told Annie that as far back as I could remember I had wanted to be a doctor, had read everything about medicine I could get my hands on. But one day in tenth-grade French class I heard a noise behind me like an outboard engine running wild out of water, it rapidly increased to a very high intensity, and I turned around, stared in horror—a friend of mine, Ronny Cooper, the son of a Lutheran minister, was stretched out between the desks, jerking in all extremities and frothing at the mouth. His eyes were rolled back until only the whites could be seen. I was terrified, so were my classmates, so was the teacher. The seizure abated. I guess the Cooper family was trying to keep Ronny's epilepsy a secret, which was why he had never been taken to a doctor for it. But after seeing that, I knew I didn't want to be a doctor. The thought of having to deal with sickness like that horrified me. The sight of a needle going into an arm made me feel like I was going to faint. So I lost my resolve until my sophomore year of college.

But in my freshman year in med school I was second in my class. I should have been first. On the gross-anatomy final we'd go from cadaver to cadaver, and a part would be tagged and you were supposed to identify it. I knew the human body, I knew it perfectly! I would have had a perfect score on that exam, except there was a squashed-down piece of body that I identified as a tendon, and lots of my friends called it a tendon, but one female student recognized it as being a squashed penis. My inability to recognize a squashed penis kept me from being at the top of my class.

Annie was pleased by that story.

We were taking turns with the driving, and she didn't need a driver's license, she needed a pilot's license. Not paying any attention at all to the road, she was telling me that she was terribly worried about two girls, June and July.

"June and July?"

"Blond twins, both of them pregnant by the end of football season. They knew how to cheer! But they didn't know how to protect themselves. And Nancy wore a navy-blue parka, nylon, all the time in class, never took it off. She was pregnant, too. But wouldn't admit it. Nancy tried out for cheerleading when she was seven months gone. The baby was born with a broken shoulder." At the wheel, Annie sighed and was silent awhile, and then she told me about Lorraine, a girl who turned tricks in a Tularosa motel during the noon hour. "I said to her, 'Girl, get off your back and come to class.' " Annie got a little mournful. "All the money went to her family." And then she said, in that wonderful non sequitur way of hers, "You should hear them, Jim, when they talk about the territories their grandparents roamed in."

The territory we were roaming in was pretty grim. A freak cold front had clamped down over everything, freezing that portion of the world with sleet, the highway like glass. On our way to Monterrey we saw some horses lying on their backs, very dead, feet in the air, covered with ice. Some of them were actually still standing up, dead, frozen to the spot. The animals were glazed. I couldn't understand why they hadn't survived, as horses in Montana will do though they experience far colder weather for a far longer period of time. Annie and I stayed the first night at a place that didn't look like much from the outside, and from the inside it looked like a lot less. The next day we pushed on to Durango, then at night on down to Mazatlán—the hotel clerk thought we were crazy, because the area was still full of robbers. Our plan was to go from Mazatlán by ferry over to the tip of Baja California, but I couldn't pass up the chance to go deep-sea fishing for marlin in Mazatlán. I had done it once before, and it was tremendously exciting. Annie was a good sport, and we went out with a little Mexican captain who managed to get us both seasick, and we didn't catch a thing. That evening, when we were ready to take the ferry, we looked at each other and knew we couldn't get on another boat and go across water, so we stopped at a little town and went out on the beach, which was infested with black flies. We moved on, but wherever we went we had an absolutely miserable time for the next three days. We drove aimlessly. One night when the car broke down we slept in it. We did somewhat better in Las Noches, but when we arrived in Tucson we had hardly sat down in a restaurant when we both became violently ill, ran to the bathrooms, and threw up, we had gotten nailed by something in Las Noches twenty-four hours before. It was looking like the worst vacation of both our lives.

But it wasn't. No, not at all. We had the nights together, and we lived for them, and they were so lovely (even that night in the car). Never before had it been for me anything like what we now were for each other. It was absolutely new and beautiful. Sometimes it made me feel like one who'd just gone through the motions before, someone who had missed the point. I guess I'd thought of sex as something you *do*. Annie brought her whole life to the bedroom, a life with such a large share of hurt and disappointment, her stories made me cringe. Her first husband, Silas's father, was Leonard Lester, firstborn son of Barnabas Lester. Leonard had been the captain of the Tularosa High basketball team (and was still the career scoring leader), Prince Charming. He didn't do much for a few years, but then he pulled himself together to become a Golden Eagle in 'Nam. Lester came back from the war to be a captain of the "Red Hats," the fire-fighting brigade of Apaches; he'd go fight a fire somewhere and return home to show Annie pictures of the woman he had fucked. Now a policeman somewhere in Texas, Leonard the alcoholic had once, in the middle of the night, beat Annie unmercifully and in the morning had no memory of what he had done.

I lay close beside her in bed and listened to her. She was so beautiful, and with each passing night we seemed to get closer. I hadn't wanted to bring marijuana to Mexico, I had a little snit fit and said they'd stop us at the border and we'd rot forever in a two-bit jail, but she had insisted and was carrying some toothpick joints in her birth-control kit. At the end of the day she'd lie all wonderfully nude on the hotel bed, inhaling a "doobie." I'd trace with my fingers the little pink scars on both her brown knees, scars from bike wrecks when she was a kid. I'd trace my way upward, and meanwhile she was tracing me, her touch desperately soft. We both knew the terrible penalties the human body takes, how complex the body is, how vulnerable. For months in that little hospital we had plunged our hands deep into ruined guts and torn flesh. We knew what a great gift physical pleasure could be; to have it seemed almost like cheating. When we fucked she would take forever getting to the top of the mountain, and her feet would cramp up, they'd stay that way for a minute or two, her toes helplessly curled, and she'd grab hold of my head, her fingers plunged into my hair, and whisper, and then burst into tears, going over the top. I'd remember the first time, at her house, the chanting chorus of Silas's "Messenger Bird." The one night we slept in the broken-down Chevy, we killed a bottle of tequila. She had to keep staggering out to pee, and a high wind would knock her over, and then she'd stumble back in, ready for anything. We were exquisitely happy.

And sex didn't stay in bed, it followed us around all day long. I was seeing things and looking at the world in a hungry new way; more sex seemed to be invested in things than I had ever suspected; I delivered myself of monumental sexual insights, and she'd play adoring audience. I'd say, behind the wheel, "I have figured out the difference between Mexican girls and Indian girls."

"You have?"

"Mexican girls swing their hips, and Indian girls don't."

"Are you sure?"

"I am. Mexican girls dance this way a little and that way a little; Indian girls tread, slowly, straight ahead. Mexican girls take *off* from the ground, but Indian girls are a little *in* the ground."

She looked at me for a long time. Then she smiled and put her hand gently on my leg.

But sometimes—I never understood how it happened, and I never understood how to prevent it—we'd just lose it, fall completely apart. What usually triggered it was when we'd be remembering our childhoods. Childhood was no picnic for either one of us. It had taken us an inordinately long time to figure people out—as if happiness were a secret, a secret nobody would let us in on. You'd think that that would be a big reason Annie and Jim were drawn to each other. And maybe it was. But Annie would be musing along about her childhood, and Jim would be visualizing her in a kind of dreamy way, when suddenly, bingo, that tone in Annie's voice would appear, and she'd say, "When you played cowboys and Indians, did you ever want to be an Indian, or did you always want to be a cowboy?" She'd look at me as if I had been, and still was, a cowboy.

I told her about my freshman year at Columbia. I was so exhilarated to be in the Big Apple—and especially to be away from home, since home was where Mom had died of the cancer we were not allowed to mention, and my father had gone into perpetual mourning, the realest emotion I'd ever seen him express. No, at seventeen I was in Morningside Heights, on my own, discovering a whole new world. One day I ran into a Black Muslim on Broadway and 116th Street, and the guy pestered me to buy a copy of *Muhammad*

Speaks. I said to him, in my teenage obtuse and hopelessly naive voice, "Why should I pay money to read that the white race was invented by a mad scientist four thousand years ago?" (Annie interrupted. "Muhammad sounds right to me.") But I would not be stopped in my story; I told her that that black guy in the black suit and black necktie said I was a "white devil" because I had inherited the "devil seed" from my great-grandfather who owned slaves. I said to him, "In Winnipeg?"

But Annie didn't get it—or didn't want to—she just shook her head. As we were coming into El Paso, I said, "Jesus, honey, you know I'm nuts about you. You got a grudge against love?"

"Yeah," she said, "I got a grudge against love. I been there before."

"Well, you sure spend a lot of time trying to decide if I'm—what?—if I'm *okay*."

She was still expressionless. Then she sighed. "Max said something to me last week."

I waited, driving.

She looked over at me. "Max said, 'Now don't you and Jimmy go falling in love. You know how we always get punished for that.' "

"Uh-huh."

She turned away and said out the window, to the arid landscape, "Think we will?"

PART Two

"THE RED INDIAN, as a civilized and truly religious man, civilized beyond taboo and totem, as he is in New Mexico, is religious in perhaps the oldest sense, and deepest, of the word. Go on some brilliant snowy morning and see the dark figure on the roof: or come riding through at dusk on some windy evening, when the black skirts of the silent women blow around the white wide boots, and you will feel the old, old root of human consciousness still reaching down to depths we know nothing of: and of which, only too often, we are jealous. Never shall I forget watching the dancers, the men with the fox-skin swaying down from their buttocks, file out and the women with seed rattles following. The long, streaming, glistening black hair of the men. Even in ancient Crete long hair was sacred in a man, as it is still in the Indians. Never shall I forget the utter absorption of the dance, so steadily, timelessly rhythmic, and silent, with the ceaseless downtread, always to the earth's centre. Never shall I forget the deep singing of the men at the drum, swelling and sinking, the deepest sound I have heard in all my life, deeper than thunder, deeper than the sound of the Pacific Ocean, deeper than the roar of the deep waterfall: the wonderful deep sound of men calling to the unspeakable depths."

—D. H. Lawrence

O NE OF THE SADDEST things about the job was the way we'd lose track of our patients. We'd discharge them from the hospital, and they'd go back out there somewhere to what they called home, and we wouldn't see them again, often not until they died. We'd think they were on the road to recovery, we had no knowledge they'd gone downhill again. And, to be honest, many times the injuries or illnesses I had to deal with were so savage, so close to the bone, that I couldn't bear to carry them in my conscious mind—my conscious mind was like a bulging file drawer where gradually the old records would get crowded out and be thrown away.

I thought I was on top of it with Tennyson Browne, a

man very proud of his name who loved to refer to himself in the third person most singular, a rich, rhetorical "Tennyson Browne." He had been coming in for years. Everything seemed to happen to Tennyson Browne. He'd get stabbed in the back with a pitchfork. He'd get into a fight and come in with broken arms and broken hands from being hit with chains. Once his daughter brought him in, saying he was possessed by devils (he'd had a fit of DTs down at the tribal store). He loved to watch old cowboy-and-Indian movies on TV—*Fort Apache* was his favorite. He always carried a Bible with him now, so God would protect him from getting beaten up all the time. He said, "God will take care of Tennyson Browne, God has his eye on Tennyson Browne." And he'd eat anything he was given—once I watched him devour an entire loaf of bread and wash it down with two big pitchers of Kool-Aid. He liked to tease the nurses about how in the good old days an unfaithful woman had the tip of her nose cut off.

But when his long-suffering wife died Tennyson Browne went even crazier than before. He had intense visions of his Peggy, surrounded by celestial radiance, and he seemed to be just letting himself die. He never took his insulin or other medicines, they were found all neatly wrapped and stored away. When he lost Peggy he might just as well have dropped dead. But it took Tennyson Browne over a year to drop dead. One day, unable to stand his sorrow any longer, he went out under a tree and slit his wrists. And his ankles. And his throat.

Wilma Lester, Barnabas's wife, kept telling him that the other nurses were always praised and she never was. So Barnabas would come over to the hospital and give us hell about it. He had already got rid of two or three people on the staff because of run-ins they'd had with Wilma. And he thought PHS doctors were arrogant young know-it-alls who were literally "practicing" medicine. On one of his visits, I was oddly touched by a drama I saw played out on his face. He said Wilma had told him about my slipshod attitude; a flu bug was going around, and Wilma had told him that I had said, "If you treat it very well and very carefully, it should last about a week; if you do nothing, it should last about seven days." Wilma had said, "He's lazy, and he doesn't care." It was only while Barnabas was repeating what I had said, saying it aloud in his own voice, that he heard my obvious irony, and he blinked, stuck. He had loved that Wilma for so long that he was always on her side; he had gotten so used to her, he almost didn't hear her anymore.

Barnabas was still in my office that day when I received an emergency call from the far eastern side of the reservation where a road crew had been digging a ditch. I got into the ambulance and hurried over there, about a thirty-minute drive, to Cloudcroft; when I got there I found that they had been using a backhoe to dig a six-foot ditch to put pipe in, and two workers who were standing in the ditch had got buried. The construction workers had been scooping desperately with their hands in the extremely soft earth; the two Apaches were standing in that ditch as though they had been planted there, just their heads sticking out of the dirt. They were blue, they were dead, their mouths full of mud, mud all over their eyes and ears, their chests had been so compressed that they couldn't expand them at all. There they stood.

That night I was on call, and four members of the tribe

came by the hospital to drop off Danny Baca in the front hall. A real hard-core drinker, Danny was a scrawny little guy with a couple of tattoos on his arms, which probably meant he had spent some time out in Los Angeles, where the Mescaleros occasionally went, to hang out there, or in San Diego with the navy boys. Danny Baca was lying on the floor of the front lobby, and he looked essentially moribund; I didn't smell alcohol on him, but he was all skin and bone, it looked like he hadn't eaten in weeks. Clearly there wasn't much time. Annie and I got him in and up on an examining table, which was easy to do since he was so frail. He could answer yes or no, and then his eyes would roll up so that only the whites stared at you. Shallow respiration, a little cough, a temperature of 104. Just by looking at him you could see that his left chest cavity was bigger than his right and seemed to bulge out; I thumped on his chest and found it absolutely filled with fluid in the left lung cavity. The right lung was still working a little, but he clearly wasn't exchanging oxygen very well. We took an X ray. He had a low white count, all of the cells were fighter cells, but it showed that the body was overwhelmed by infection. When I touched his chest wall he would flinch, and the area felt comparatively warm to me. I'd never seen anything like it before, but I knew at once what it was— an empyema. He had a big abscess in his left chest cavity; his pneumonia had gotten out of control, and the germs had seeped through the lining of the lung and into the chest cavity itself. A boil the size of a football. Now I knew where all those little white cells were.

I put him on his right side with his left side pointing toward the ceiling. I made about a one-inch incision between his ribs, just a hair above the heart and to the left. As the knife cut down through the tissue between the intercostal muscles, pus spumed out of him, it actually went all the way up to the ceiling (later we had to have one of the janitors clean it). The odor was horrendous. This was evidently an anaerobic bacteria, which lives without oxygen and creates a tremendous amount of gas and pus; it cleared everybody but me out of the vicinity for some period of time. After this initial volcanic action had subsided, I stuffed a great big rubber catheter in there, cut a couple of extra holes in it, and over the next five minutes I took out over a liter and a half of purulent foul-smelling gunk. Danny Baca began to perk up a little. He said, "Doc, that feels a *lot* better."

I loaded him up with streptomycin and penicillin, and much to my amazement Danny Baca did get better. He had to be on oxygen for two weeks. His buddies would come in to visit (and he got started back on alcohol even before he got out of the hospital). What you do in a case like that is back the tube off a little bit each day, so that the cavity gradually closes in, without leaving any space for a residual infection; I also had the tube on suction to keep the lung expanded. I was slowly, slowly backing it out, and when there were two inches left Danny Baca finished the job. He gave us a surly look and said he couldn't understand why anybody needed to be in the hospital for two whole weeks. He said white man's medicine seemed to help, but it sure took a long time.

About this time we caught our first blizzard, one hell of a snow; I had been watching the clouds gather, the whole sky piled high. Ever since I had first arrived I had loved to look at that New Mexico sky, its vastness; in the summer those thunderstorms would gather down at the end of the valley and prepare for the march up the valley. When they'd hit we'd have a power outage, and I'd have to go down into the basement to play with the backup emergency generator. But this time it was the wet, cold white stuff. Pita told me she'd heard on the radio that the Tularosa schools were starting to bus the Indian students home before the blizzard completely closed the roads. In the pelting snow I went down to meet the bus, both Annie and Silas were on it, and we had to abandon my Chevy about halfway up their road and do the last hundred yards on foot. I didn't mind because it was all so beautiful, and I was happy to be cooped up with my family. Silas seemed to be having a little difficulty at school, so I helped him with his biology homework. He said he didn't see any reason to learn this shit, he'd never use it. I thought about that, and then I said he would use it, he'd have to use it, if he chose a career that I knew he could do beautifully. He said, "What's that?" I had his full attention, and I whispered, "Pediatrics." A wonderful smile took possession of his features, and we talked for hours as the snow kept falling out there, burying Mescalero.

One bitterly cold night, Lucinda Carillo, a lovely sixteen-year-old Apache girl, truly put Max Rubenstein to the test. The previous summer Lucinda had turned fifteen, and it had been time for her coming-out party. Between July 1 and July 5, the Mescalero custom was to celebrate the new debutantes. The girls would make their own dresses of soft home-tanned buckskin. The parents provided all the food for the feast; the girls were kept under guard in their own tents, though they made appearances sporadically throughout the festival. After four days of celebration the girls became women. Lucinda Carillo was quite lovely, and the following fall she was in Annie's homeroom and history class. Lucinda went out for cheerleading, even though few of the Indian girls did. Lucinda was beautiful, bright, and determined to go on to the University of New Mexico; Annie spent many an extra hour tutoring her.

That winter night Lucinda came into the clinic bruised and disheveled, her clothes all torn, one breast lacerated; she was in shock, clutching her body, and between sobs she told her story. Robert Swanson and Charlie Francis, two Anglo boys, had offered her a ride home. They took her to a back road, dragged her from the car, tore off her clothes, and took turns raping her. Robert threatened her with a long narrow switchblade; he said he'd cut off her tits or cut off her cunt if she so much as squirmed. (This practice was not without precedent; a hundred years earlier, American soldiers had done exactly that in a massacre of a Sioux village—they had amputated the vulvas of Sioux women and stuck them on their saddle horns as mementos.) Lucinda said that in a parting gesture Robert had rammed his knife up her vagina.

Max wasted no time. He quickly did an upright film of the abdomen; he could see air under the diaphragm, a sure sign that the intestine had been perforated; he washed out her abdominal cavity and repaired the rents in her uterus and small intestine. The knife had apparently missed the other vital organs, though there was some bruising of the pancreas. Max felt that he could get by without drains— he wanted as inconspicuous a scar as possible—and he was confident that she'd do well. But Lucinda Carillo did not do well. She got sicker, with a high fever; a mass developed in her midabdomen. A lab test showed that she had pancreatitis. Surgeons are dreadfully afraid of the pancreas because when it becomes inflamed, in this case from injury, all those good pancreatic juices come out into the abdominal cavity and begin to digest everything in sight, the kidneys, the gut, the fat, blood vessels. They can digest all of your intra-abdominal contents and kill you. To compound things, this was happening in an abdomen contaminated with bacteria, and Lucinda had developed a pancreatic abscess, a condition that is 100 percent fatal unless drained. Max had no options. He had to go back in. He put in a G-tube and all sorts of drains. He had to leave the wound open, and now this lovely young woman had a gaping slash down into her abdomen. Max asked me to look at her, and I did; everything that could be done was being done. She was on all the right antibiotics. But I knew she'd be dead in a week. It would be slow and it would be agonizing.

I followed Annie in to watch her change the dressings. Lucinda's mother, Juanita, was sitting there holding her hand, squeezing very tightly because it hurt so bad. Juanita was looking the other way because she would be sick if she watched, as I almost was. The wound was six inches long and three inches wide; what you saw was a cauldron, like a volcano of yellowish cloudy bile bubbling up, about a quart and a half coming out every day. You could see abdominal organs, intestines, the edge of the liver, even the kidneys, all fibrous and covered with a slimy yellow cream. You knew that pancreatic juice was just eating everything away. If it ate through a big blood vessel, Lucinda would die in minutes.

Every day Max had to go in and see it, to watch it and know that if he'd used drains in the first place it probably wouldn't have happened. He had to live with it and yet carry on with his usual practice. A surgeon goes through agony when he thinks he's really screwed somebody up. But for all his lovely kindness, Max had ice water in his veins, absolute ice water for blood. I could never, never do it; to make rounds and see that and then go on and do another case. I don't think I'd have the balls.

A month later, though, Lucinda was still alive, steadily improving, and ready to go home. Perhaps luck, perhaps Apache toughness. Robert Swanson and Charlie Francis were arrested and tried in Alamogordo, charged with aggravated assault; both were sent to the federal penitentiary. The good people of Tularosa and Alamogordo, however, were outraged that their sons could be sent to jail for something so trivial as trying to have fun with an Indian girl.

▲ ▲ ▲ ▲ ▲ ▲ ▲ ▲ ▲ ▲ ▲ ▲ ▲ ▲ ▲ ▲ ▲ ▲

WAS FLYING BACK TO El Paso from a medical conference I had attended in San Diego. My companion in the next seat was a proper woman of about forty, and when lunch came we were having a nice quiet conversation. Halfway through lunch, she said, "Oh, *shit!*" That seemed a little peculiar, coming from her, and so I asked her what the trouble was. She said, "I just ate a peanut." I said, "What happens when you eat peanuts?"

She said, "Well, I get all swollen up, my tongue gets swollen, I get hives, and I can't breathe." I said oh. I said, "Did you bring your medicine with you?" She said, "No, I left it at home, I sort of came at the last minute." While

I was talking with her I was buzzing the stewardess, and when she came I asked her to bring the medicine kit that all airlines have. I looked through it and found sufficient bandages to cover a platoon, but no useful medicine. Within two or three minutes, the woman, true to her word, was covered with hives, her tongue was swelling, her eyes were swollen shut, and she was beginning to have trouble breathing. I got on the P.A. and asked if there were any asthmatics on board; I thought I could use one of their Isuprel inhalers. A couple of people responded, so I went to work on the woman. Isuprel will work like a shot of adrenaline and reverse the anaphylactic shock she was going into. Various passengers offered me Benadryl, steroids, prednisone; an eager-to-help young guy in the seat immediately behind us offered me cocaine. I gave the lady some medication, and within five minutes she clearly began to feel better. So did I. Then she collapsed, and I spent the rest of the flight— we were at 35,000 feet—ministering over her as she lay in the aisle. She was conscious and able to breathe. The pilot, who was wonderful, came back and asked if I wanted to land immediately, and I said I thought we should just head for El Paso. I kept trying to get the lady to sit up, but she would get faint when she did, so we sandbagged her in the aisle and made it to El Paso, a supersmooth landing. An ambulance was waiting for us, and I presume she was fine. I was puzzled that I never heard from her, but she probably didn't remember or at the time was unable to comprehend what was going on. The airline sent me a note with fifty bucks enclosed. I sent them back a very long letter, explaining that this was a situation that could happen very easily and that they might consider supplying their medical kits with four or five absolutely necessary drugs. (And they did it! Within two months they had their flights supplied with kits that included some rescue drugs.)

I felt very sad, though, my next day back at the hospital. An old Indian lady brought her twenty-year-old daughter into the clinic; the daughter had little white stars pasted onto her forehead. She was one of the very few youngsters on the reservation who had gone on to college, up to UNM in Albuquerque, but her high intelligence had been blind-sided by some emotional malady. This girl had really run off the tracks; apparently she had taken on a whole frater-nity house one night, fucked all the brothers, and was found the next morning walking aimlessly around the campus in torn, ragged clothes. She had been put in the clinic there, then prematurely discharged. We sat in the little examining room, and the girl seemed quite happy, blithely telling me she had a radio in her head and the radio played all her professors' lectures to her. She could go to college without ever having to be there! I glanced over at the mother, and tears were very slowly making their way down her cheeks.

I had no experience whatsoever in dealing with this kind of case; I figured it would take a real psychiatrist. It was about the only case I saw in Mescalero where I des-perately wanted a shrink to come in and treat a personal, individual case of severe emotional disorder. There were, in abundance, people with all sorts of "mental illness." But the illnesses seemed to me social and cultural. Political. How does a psychiatrist "cure" the chronically unemployed, or the resulting alcoholism and despair? Old Barnabas Les-ter—in his court battles involving the reservation's timber contracts, mining rights, his efforts to push everything through for the "Ski Apache" up on Sierra Blanca—Christ,

in the courtroom that man was curing a lot more "illness"
than I was in the hospital. I even said that to him once,
when I ran into him on a twilight stroll along Warbonnet
Road (he was walking that dumb porcupine-chasing dog
he was so fond of). Quietly I told him what I had been
thinking, and his eyes suddenly went far away somewhere;
it was an emotion I would have thought he never felt, a
kind of immense wild sorrow. But just for that moment.
Then he was Chief Barnabas Lester again, annoyed by what
he realized he had let me see.

"WE FOUND AMONG THE SIOUX little evidence of individual conflicts, inner tensions, or of what we call neuroses—anything which would have permitted us to apply our knowledge of mental hygiene, such as it was, to a solution of the Indian problem. What we found was cultural pathology, sometimes in the form of alcoholic delinquency or of mild thievery, but for the most part in the form of a general apathy and an intangible passive resistance against any further and more final impact of white standards on the Indian conscience."

—Erik Erikson, *Childhood and Society*

▲ ▲ ▲ ▲ ▲ ▲ ▲ ▲ ▲ ▲ ▲ ▲ ▲ ▲ ▲ ▲ ▲ ▲ ▲ ▲

N THE MIDDLE OF his junior year, eleventh grade, Silas decided to drop out of school. He was doing very poorly in his courses. Annie was heartbroken. And shocked, for she hadn't seen it coming. And, too, she said she felt more than a little betrayed; she was, after all, a member of the Tularosa High faculty, and not one of her colleagues had come to her with news about how deep a hole Silas was digging himself into. Then she switched— yes, they had told her, two teachers had issued subtle warnings, but she was so wrapped up in the boy that she had failed to listen.

I felt like a stranger to both of them. Worse, they had suddenly become strangers to each other. All of Silas's life, he and his mom had been allies, ever since Leonard used to take turns abusing them. And after that sonofabitch was out of the picture mother and son had continued to become, over the years, beautifully and unnaturally close. But now it was goddamn war.

In my office one day, Annie said, "What he's doing is such a personal rejection of *me*."

"Why?"

"*Why?* Jim, don't you see that dropping out of school is a rejection of everything I stand for?"

Before I could catch myself, I put into words what worried me, that he'd lose his student deferment, which would most likely mean he'd get caught in the draft. Poor Annie hadn't got to that one yet, and when I said it a look of absolute panic came over her face. Then, in a minute, her eyes narrowed, and she muttered, "Shit, he'll go to Vietnam just like his father." It was all I could do to snap my fingers and say, "Oh, what am I talking about? He's only seventeen, we've got time to work it out."

At first Silas backpedaled. He said, "It's not my intention not to graduate."

His mom tried to distance herself with a little sarcasm. She said, "Now, dear, don't use a double negative."

He said, "I didn't."

Annie ran the sentence through her mind again and looked at me.

I looked at the floor. In the weeks to come I would spend a lot of my time looking at the floor.

The only class Silas liked at all was French, and he promised to continue his French in summer school. He genuinely admired Mr. Noblett, the chairman of the languages department. "His presence," Silas said, in that funny way of his, "is very light."

From my one and only talk with Mr. Noblett, I thought he was a kind of superannuated hippie, but Silas said the man had integrity and strength of character. Everybody else at that school, save his darling ma, was a waste of time. "They're all a bunch of assholes!"

"They are not," his mother said. "You can't go through your life thinking the rest of the world is a bunch of assholes."

Silas smirked. "Okay, I'll go through my life thinking the way you do, that they're unwitting instruments of the capitalist system."

Annie didn't like that one bit, and they were off and running. Anger was the usual emotion in her face, but sometimes I saw a terrible fear. I'm pretty sure that she was seeing in Silas an old story, Indian lethargy and self-destructiveness. Just another Apache dropout. And she couldn't bear that. Maybe she saw his father in him.

It was extremely painful for all three of us. The arguments usually ended with Silas going to his room, slamming the door, and pacing around in there like a madman. Then he'd emerge to growl, "I have to go for a walk." And he would do that. One bitter evening I stood out on the icy deck and watched him trudge all the way down into the valley, then over toward the big Catholic mission. He took an hour, and it was *cold* out there.

Annie was furiously processing it all; each day she'd have a fresh line of attack, or a little volley like "How can you, you who enjoy so much your teaching in Head Start—how can you drop out of school? Some role model you are for your kids!" And Silas was doing the same thing, opening his own lines of attack. "Leave me alone—you *drink* too much. You get drunk every night!" Which was not true, but there was truth in it, Annie was so unhappy that she was hitting the bottle awfully hard.

In early May a truce was achieved. Mother and son worked together and drafted a formal letter to the principal, setting out Silas's plans for summer school and then for the fall semester. They went over it and handed it to me for my opinion; it was full of promises and schedules and pro- posed conferences with an adviser. Under these rules Silas would be allowed to audit the rest of the current school year, as a gesture of good faith, and then would start taking courses for credit in the coming fall. His mother would monitor his progress. But the whole thing fell through in a week. The English teacher tossed Silas out of her class, and all he'd say was that Mrs. Davis was an idiot. "She was trying to explain the difference between 'fearful' and 'fear- some.' She said, 'He was fearful to her.' Bitch can't even understand her own examples."

It was the same with all his courses. Silas was so busy fighting that he didn't have any time left over to learn.

Annie quit the sauce. She did a damn good job of staying away from it, and I was real proud of her, but she suffered agonizing insomnia. Irritable all the time. One morning, after a bad quarrel at breakfast, Silas just looked at her and said softly, "What do you want me to do?" She stared at him and then fairly screamed, *"Wash the dishes!"*

One night in late August (after that charade of summer school had fallen through) Silas fled, with his sleeping bag and a lantern, into a cornfield. I was appointed to get him back, and I followed his trail in there as best I could, calling his name. Next day he said to me, "Wow, Jim, you kept *just* missing me, your steps going crash, crash, crash, and then I looked up to see you peering through the tall stalks of corn at my abandoned lantern."

The boy wasn't mean, but he was. The boy wasn't lazy, but he was. Even casual little things, which before had seemed loving, now became little chapters of menace. One night we were having a fairly innocent discussion—about Plato, as I recall, why poets were banished from his republic—and Silas bent down to capture a moth. He took it, cupped in his hands, to the open door and flung it to the night. "Fly, little friend, fly and be free." Even those gentle words seemed harnessed to some vague aggression. He sat himself down, looked at his mother, and explained, "Lepidoptera."

Annie was helpless; Silas was isolated. His failure at French had seemed to me virtually guaranteed, since inordinate time and trouble had been sunk into that course. How do you learn a foreign language when so much has been invested in just getting you there, physically, seated in the classroom? Mainly I felt afraid for them, and terribly inadequate myself. I couldn't help. One night Annie screwed up, she fell into the hooch again, and after we'd got her to bed Silas and I went down and sat on the ground beside the pond, listening to the frogs and insects. I said to him that I'd never met anybody else who was so bright and imaginative, who by every fiber and implication of his being *belonged* in school. I came on a little strong; I said that his dropping out of school struck me as an act of self-mutilation. I had trouble saying the word "self-mutilation," and Silas didn't much enjoy hearing it. Then we were silent for a while, staring up at the wild canopy of stars. Finally Silas said, "I didn't realize how desperate Mom really was. Not until Grandpa called. He had me come to his big house for lunch."

"Well, it's understandable that a concerned grandfather would take a keen interest in the welfare—"

Silas burst out laughing.

I smiled a little, looking at him. "What? What?"

"Oh," he said, "listen to yourself. Did you hear the words you just said? 'A concerned grandfather would take a keen interest in the welfare' . . ." And he lay back on the ground still laughing.

I felt like a fool. I said, "Lepidoptera."

"What?"

"Right."

He sat up again. "Anyway—it just seemed to me so bizarre that Mom would take the problem to Grandpa. I mean, they don't exactly get along."

"Why do you think that is?"

He paused. "Politics." He looked at me. "In the deepest sense of the word."

"Well, then, tell me."

"Tell you what?"

"Jesus, Silas, sometimes I think you *have* fried your brain. What did Barnabas say to you?"

Silas sighed and put his arms around his knees. "He said that if I stayed in school and graduated he'd buy me a car."

I pondered the deal.

"But I really fucking zapped him."

"You did?"

"Oh, yeah, man. I sat there staring at my salad—oh, it was perfect—I slowly looked up at my grandfather, and I said, 'What kind of car?' " Silas laughed helplessly. "Oh, you should have seen his *face!*"

So our problems didn't exactly get fixed; our problems just wore us out. Annie especially. At the hospital, she did her job mechanically, rather poorly, amidst odd little catnaps in my office. She had a slight limp, and she said, "You know, I think I've got tendinitis or something." Her left hip was really sore, and it continued to hurt. I thought perhaps she had developed bursitis. So I injected the trochanteric bursa over the hip with a little cortisone. That seemed to help.

But Annie's hip pain appeared trivial when one man was brought into the ER; he had been loading a train, and by some mishap lost his footing and fell right between two cars just as they coupled. The couplers got him in midback and midabdomen. When the ambulance brought him in he was still alive, and he seemed like such a nice man, lying there stunned, not in very much pain. He had a hole the size of a football in his abdomen, all the way through, you could see light through this guy. Both kidneys were crushed, the aorta was crushed, the pancreas was crushed, his backbone broken, his spinal cord severed, every organ smashed beyond repair. But all he did was lie there with that bewildered look on his face, unchanging, even when he died.

B▲▲▲▲▲▲▲▲▲▲▲▲▲▲▲▲▲▲
ACK IN LATE FEBRUARY, I had looked
out my office window one day to see a crowd of people,
most of them men, marching up the hill toward the hospital.
They looked like an approaching army. One of them came
into the hospital and told a nurse that we should get ready
for an emergency. A woman had called the sheriff to report
her twenty-two-month-old daughter was missing. One of
the child's mittens had been found in the driveway. The
little girl's name was Christina Clark, and I had treated her
a few months earlier when she had been suffering from
some minor viral infection. But what I remembered most
was the vivid contrast in coloring between her and her
mother. Christina looked pure Apache, with her jet-black

hair and bright little black eyes; her mother, Patricia, was a very fair-skinned blonde. I didn't recall whether Patty was divorced from the child's father, but I knew they were not living together; Patty had told me, in her roundabout way, that she was stuck at home with the baby all the time and was getting by on welfare.

Now I went to the other side of the hospital and looked up to where the search party was beginning to comb the snowy hillside; Mrs. Clark's little house was up there somewhere, and the dozens of volunteers were trying to find the child before she succumbed to exposure in the cold. Along about midafternoon they called off their efforts there and decided to search an area around the father's house over by Apache Summit.

A radio station had received a phone call requesting a song, and during the brief conversation the male caller was heard shushing a child in the background: "Be quiet, Christina." And a man who managed a package store in Alamogordo called the sheriff to say he had seen a little girl resembling the description of Christina; when he had tried to talk to her she ran away.

The next day the story was in the paper and on our local TV news. Christina's father, Floyd Clark, had passed a lie-detector test. Photographs of Christina were shown, and the district attorney came on camera to say he would recommend leniency if the toddler was returned unharmed. Patty made an extremely agitated plea for the return of her daughter. Each day we were treated to something. Patty was estranged not only from her husband but also from her family in Albuquerque. When she married an Indian, she was told by her mother that she no longer would be thought of as a daughter. When Christina was born, Patty's parents sent a funeral wreath. But the trouble had really started way back in Patty's childhood. She had dropped out of high school, apparently had passed a few bad checks, and some old family friend was quoted as saying Patty used to jump out of her second-story window. The media pounced on the story, every little detail. As I look back, I can see that it was the first of a whole string of Mescalero accidents and tragedies that dominated public attention for several months.

Patty generated considerable sympathy for herself by her sobbing pleas on TV for Christina's safe return. Floyd had provided no support for his wife and child. And, to my surprise, Annie suspected the mother; Annie was sure that the whole kidnapping business was a fraud. But a few days later Patty received in the mail the other mitten, matching the one found in the driveway. The police tried, and failed, to trace the envelope. At home beside me, Annie was conscience stricken; she kept muttering, "How could I have missed that one so bad? I was *sure*." And now all her maternal energy was marshaled into sympathy for Patty.

The breakthrough came on the thirteenth day. The police had a tape recording on which Patty seemed to say that she knew where the child was. An unnamed witness had come forward to report seeing Patty pausing for several moments at the mailbox in front of our little Mescalero post office, she seemed to be debating with herself whether or not to mail a big envelope in her hands. From that point on, the whole kidnapping story rapidly unraveled; Patty had mailed the pink mitten to herself. Now she insisted that on the morning of the disappearance she had found Christina all tangled in blankets, dead in her crib. Patty had panicked, thinking no one would believe the truth—

nobody, she said, had ever believed her, she always got blamed for things that weren't her fault. She rambled on, childhood memories of a burglary at her parents' home, missing money from her brother's room, a bottle of booze given to a relative against her parents' wishes. She had made up the kidnapping story while she was hiding Christina under a pile of brush in the woods a half-mile from her house. She had put Christina's body in a big garbage bag.

A prominent pathologist from El Paso was present at the autopsy. Christina had three minor injuries—a bruise on her forehead, scrapes on the inside of her right cheek, and a scrape on the outside of her left cheek. Her congested blood vessels and the discoloration of her brain were characteristic of acute asphyxia. The microscopic studies of tissue revealed tiny hemorrhages in her neck, suggesting trauma there before death. She seemed to have been in perfect health; I knew from my past observation of her that she was developmentally advanced, even able to pedal a tricycle, which you do not usually expect until a child is somewhat older.

By now, of course, Annie had reverted back to her original position. And I concurred. On the death certificate he wrote "asphyxia caused by some other person(s)." Christina had been smothered. In cases of SIDS (sudden infant death syndrome) estimates suggest that 25 percent may be victims of suffocation, but SIDS occurs in infants, not two-year-olds. Two-year-olds just don't get trapped in blankets; they beat themselves out or move or wiggle enough to get free.

In all events, Patty was charged with "second-degree murder, falsely reporting an incident, and obstructing governmental administration." At the trial in mid-May I had to report, as did three other prosecution witnesses, that Patty's story was medically unlikely. A board-certified specialist in anatomical and neural pathology demonstrated that it was virtually impossible for Christina to have died the way that her mother said she had; this physician used the actual crib blankets to show that even if all three of the blankets were on top of Christina she could have survived. Two relatives (on the Indian side of the family) testified that they never saw Christina get tangled in blankets or have trouble breathing or sleeping.

The little courtroom in Ruidoso was packed; about half the spectators were Anglos and half of them Indians. The case ignited intense racial feelings; before Christina's Apache aunt was ruled out of order, she said, "No way an Indian mother could have done this!" Apparently Patty's own mother and father had decided that she was their daughter again, and they both sat in the front row, directly behind her at the defense table. Two Anglo women, friends of Patty from her old job at the Alamogordo K-mart, testified that she was a good mother. One of them took pains to emphasize that Patty was an extremely warm and loving mother, always hugging Christina and holding her. "I never saw her hit her," the woman said. And she added, "How many mothers have their child's baby book caught up to date for two years and have the book sitting on the night-stand?" Unfortunately, under cross-examination the district attorney pointed out that the witness was facing charges of embezzlement in connection with her K-Mart job; she had helped her friends get free merchandise so that they could return the items for a cash refund. The D.A. said, "That says a lot about what you're willing to do for your friends." The woman left the courtroom in tears.

Still, there was no proof of motive, no evidence of foul play. The defense attorney produced a letter that Patty had written in jail to Floyd: "No matter how angry you are at me, you know how much I loved our darling baby and wouldn't hurt her. Crissy was the one thing that you and I could show that we did something good in our lives." Patty herself was on the witness stand for three hours. Christina's crib was brought in, and Patty showed how she wrapped the baby. Patty's voice quivered and quaked; tears ran down her cheeks. She spoke in the present tense, as if Christina were still alive.

But the D.A. had one last witness. The matron at the jail testified that while Patty was kneeling at Christina's coffin she whispered, "Why couldn't you just lay down and go to sleep? No, you have to fool around like you always do. Damnit, why couldn't you just go to sleep?"

After the jurors were sequestered, the first thing they did, it was reported, was pray. They were out for seven hours. When they returned, Patty sat with her eyes shut, clenching her hands. She let out a big sob of relief when she heard the foreman say that she was not guilty beyond a reasonable doubt of second-degree murder. Her defense attorney bowed his head to the table. But then the foreman went on to read that Patricia Clark was guilty of second-degree manslaughter, guilty of falsely reporting her daughter missing, and guilty of interfering with the investigation. Patty's mother went up and the two women embraced, sobbing together. Then Patty was handcuffed and taken away.

At the sentencing, Patricia Clark was given the maximum penalty, five to fifteen years in state prison. The judge said, "Christina was the most innocent of victims. Her mother did not seek medical help, lied in reporting the girl missing, and then stood by for days as dozens of concerned citizens combed the area in freezing weather. If your baby died by accident, you wouldn't stick her in a garbage bag and hide her body in the bushes."

The following fall, when the reservation was turned into an armed camp, the story of Christina and Patricia Clark was something that many of our visitors recalled. "Mescalero" was where a white woman had killed her Apache baby.

" 'WHAT FOR YOU SHOOT?' she said. 'What Huron do, dat you kill him? What you t'ink Manitou *say?* What you t'ink Manitou *feel?* What Iroquois *do?* No get honor—no get camp—no get prisoner—no get battle—no get scalp—no get not'ing at all. Blood come after blood! You big as great pine—Huron gal little slender birch— why you fall on her and crush her? You t'ink Huron forget it? No; red-skin never forget. Why you so wicked, great pale-face?' "

—James Fenimore Cooper, *The Deerslayer*

▲ ▲

D R O V E   N O R T H   F O R   about thirty miles up into the mountains to fish. It was a lovely little stream that had some awfully nice trout in it, a fish found only in that particular stream, a native subspecies of cutthroat trout. The stream was crystal clear, just ten feet across but wide enough in spots so that you could fish with a dry fly; the biggest trout were only about seven or eight inches, they just didn't get any bigger. The skies clouded up, it began to rain, and I decided to give it up. Driving back down toward the valley, I saw a very bedraggled man sitting on the side of the road; he looked like he'd been hitchhiking but was now so tired and exhausted he had stopped sticking his thumb out. He looked about fifty; with a poncho over his shoulders, wearing a cowboy hat and cowboy boots, he sat all curled up at the side of the road. I stopped and asked him if he wanted to get in out of the rain. He said that would be wonderful. He climbed into the front seat of the Chevy, and away we went.

He looked awful. Pale, shivering, he told me he was a cowboy from Montana and he was getting too old for the business. He said he'd been thrown hundreds of times; now he had been in some sort of rodeo competition up there, and he had not done very well. He was going to Mexico to ply his trade. Covered with grit and dust and mud and a five days' growth of beard, the guy had been getting little rides here and there all the way down from Big Falls. For the past two or three days he'd felt terrible, couldn't seem to eat. He said, "My balls swole up so big I can't walk nowhere." After his last rodeo he'd gone out on a fling with a whore, and he wondered if she had passed something on to him.

I took him to the hospital, had the nurses clean him up, and indeed his left testicle was about the size of a grapefruit. I did a urethral smear and found that he had gonorrhea. Through the microscope I could see the body's little white fighters, they had engulfed a number of these little gram-negative organisms. They're a cinch to treat with penicillin. But gonorrhea doesn't always give you just a puslike discharge; it can infect the epididymis, as it had in this old cowboy, or it can infect a joint in your body and make you extremely sick. All things considered, my having picked him up was a great deal for my lonesome wrangler—he was safe and warm and dry in a hospital where he didn't have to pay. I gave him lots of penicillin over the next few days, and his testes shrank back down to the size of a golf ball. He was a new man. He had been riding in rodeos since he was a kid, and just out of curiosity I x-rayed his chest; he had six rib fractures on the left, eight rib fractures on the right, a deformed humerus in the right arm, eight compression fractures in the back (he must have been a lot shorter now than when he started). As he set out south to Mexico, he was extremely grateful. And Uncle Sam never knew a thing about it.

During that summer we experienced a severe drought, everything dry, and for a period of three days a large forest fire raged over the eastern part of the reservation. The Mescalero Apaches weren't fighting fires as much as they used to, but they were still damn good. I was in the clinic one afternoon, there wasn't much happening, and I was curious about what a forest fire was really like. I made some excuses about being on the scene so I could take care of anybody who got hurt. Then I hopped into my Chevy and away I went. This big fire was toward the northeastern corner of the reservation, and I found myself in a maze of little dirt roads, all unnamed and unmarked, going in various directions. I could see where the smoke was coming from, and I made it to the command station. You could see fire raging along a ridge and all of a sudden jump the road and be on the other side of you, coming up behind you. The Apaches were dealing with this very calmly, apparently with no concern at all, but I was terrified. I went out on one of the lines where they were containing the fire, and I could see that this was very dangerous work indeed. Since I didn't come across any sick or hurting Indians, I scurried back to my car. I never told Annie that in the billowing smoke and sheets of fire I got lost. I went over one road after another, not knowing which way I was going;

I envisioned being found several days later, a smoked doctor in a smoldering car. After more than two hours of panic I finally felt secure again, driving down a paved road, out of danger. But for two days I coughed up this black gunky stuff. Those Apache "Red Hats" were really something; given the dangers they were exposed to, they were remarkably cool about the job.

One evening soon thereafter I drove Silas down to county court in Tularosa. The cops had stopped him on his motorcycle for speeding and discovered that he had no insurance and no registration. There were several Indian kids on the docket that night, and we gave one of them a lift back to the rez. He was the meanest kid I'd ever met, his eyes hard and distant; he sported a perpetual sneer, almost a snarl, on his face. He saw me as just a ride home, or almost home, for none of the kids to whom I gave lifts would allow me to see where they lived. I'd always drop them off at a place on the highway. With Silas, this boy, Carl, was so interesting, so bright; he seemed to love to talk, about ideas, about music, about being an Indian. Carl wanted to get off the reservation and make it big in the world. He was a fierce little guy, and I saw him a week later in the ER at the hospital when he was brought in after a fight with a terrible cut along the inside of his right forearm, the nerves had been severed, and he had no sensation or movement at all in his right hand. Max put his nerves back together and then put a big cast on him, and it had to stay there for a long time. Carl struck me as the epitome of these young Indians caught in an awful dilemma: great potential and little hope. His father had died a few years before I arrived, found with two buddies one January morning dead under some trees. They had sat out there drinking themselves into a stupor. By the time their families found them they had frozen to death.

Silas and Annie and I celebrated the return of the confiscated motorcycle: a pig roast, lots of beer for Silas and me, marijuana for Annie, and we all mellowed considerably. Silas brought out his guitar and sang for us some of his "Forty-niner" songs. They always made me feel a little disoriented anyway, and with a few beers added on I had considerable trouble finding the appropriate emotion; the lyrics were extremely funny, and then not funny at all; Silas himself seemed to be jumping around from this feeling to that feeling, grunting sarcastically and then suddenly lyrical:

> *"Passerby says: 'How, big chief,*
> *What's your beef?'*
> *Ugh, ugh, big chief, how, how.*
> *Nio, yana-yanay, hi-oh.*
>
> *"Heyah-heya, weyah-weya,*
> *Give me whiskey, honey,*
> *Suta, mni wakan,*
> *I do love you,*
> *Heya-heyah."*

Silas clearly did have a future in music; he was enormously talented and skillful. After he put his guitar away, I sat watching mother and son talk. They had patched up their quarrel, somehow, and now they were together again. I sat there, and they were just folding big laundry and conversing in a slow, easy, back-and-forth way. Something about their conversation put me a little in awe. Poor Silas had been shot down by his girlfriend, and he was feeling the baffled pain that comes over a guy when that happens. His girl had had an unfortunate experience—she had let Jesus come into her life. And now she felt that she and Silas were "living in sin." Before her conversion she had been *so* warm and affectionate; now she was *so* cold and distant. The whole thing had really thrown Silas off stride.

Annie's little comments were brief and right to the point. I could see again why so many patients in the hospital asked for her. As Silas responded to her questions, he gradually got hold of the experience and was not just a helpless victim of it. He talked quite frankly about things a guy his age usually can't get to or is too embarrassed to put into words. He'd stop and sigh over little things that weren't little at all—"Her touch was so *soft.*" He'd say it, clearly, just like that, and Annie would nod, calmly serious. She was gently coaxing him to explore the real, buried feelings that held the experience together. I couldn't quite figure out how she was doing it; I knew that whenever people's real feelings were involved Annie was a lot smarter than me. And I loved her for it.

What troubled me, though, and I knew it troubled her, too, was that our sex life had really deteriorated. It was not at all what it had been on our trip to Mexico. We didn't even do anymore a part that I had been especially fond of, at the very beginning, when I would slowly take her clothes off. Now she did it. She disrobed pretty fast and always talked while she did it (whereas before, when I had done it, neither of us spoke a word). Now it was all abrupt, hurried, as if she were saying, well, now we are going to fuck, here we are, we're taking off our clothes, and this is something we do. Like the dishes. She was oddly modest now, I hardly ever got to see her; she'd climb into bed and

pull the quilt up over her, and we'd do it in the dark, as
if she were ashamed of it. I couldn't get rambunctious at
all, I'd feel her whole body flinch.

This had been going on ever since she started having
that painful bursitis in her hips. Finally I took an X ray,
and, my God, I found a malignant lesion in her pelvis where
the hip fitted in. It was eating away the bone. I looked her
over very carefully, stark naked from nose to toes. On the
sole of her foot was a small black mole. Max removed it
and sent it, along with Annie, to El Paso. It was a malignant
melanoma. We got a bone scan, which showed lesions in a
lot of other places that hadn't started hurting yet. I kept
telling her that I just wanted to run all the relevant tests,
and I didn't tell her the results; I was hoping to find something, anything, to contradict what I was seeing. It was a
melanoma metastasizing to the bones; it would just knock
off one bone after another. Most probably it would first
cause a pelvic fracture, then multiple spinal fractures, rib
fractures, hip fractures. It would spread to the lungs, the
liver, and the brain. Melanomas are untreatable. It would
strike everywhere, and there would be no way we could
keep up with it. Radiation to each location would be ineffective; in a matter of months she wouldn't be able to sit
or lie down in any position without excruciating pain.

I did not know how or when to tell her. And I wasn't
sure that she herself didn't know. She didn't ask me. But
her eyes did. She had such a terrified, pleading look, fixing
her glance on me as if to say please, please don't confirm
what I already know. Once she said about something, jok-
ingly, "I feel it in my bones," and then, hearing what she
had said, she shot a look of terror at me.

During that time we were playing a lot of bridge—

Max and Annie against Silas and me. One night we sat at
our little card table in front of the fireplace, everybody lost
in their own thoughts. I knew I was going to have to tell
Annie the truth, and I knew it was going to be soon. I
dreaded it so. On a hand that Silas could have played as a
lay-down in three no trump, I had to struggle through in
four hearts; everything worked, I made the contract. Annie
sighed, reached out, and patted my hand. "Well, Jimmy,
you played the bejesus out of that one."

I looked at her. Annie Messenger Bird, her eyes, my
Annie looking back at me.

PART THREE

"THE CONGRESS OF THE Confederate States has passed a law declaring extermination to all hostile Indians. You will therefore use all means to persuade the Apaches to come in for the purpose of making peace, and when you get them together kill all the grown Indians and take the children prisoners and sell them to defray the expense. Buy whiskey and such other goods as may be necessary."

—Confederate Governor John R. Baylor to the commander of the Arizona Guards, 1862

▲ ▲ ▲ ▲ ▲ ▲ ▲ ▲ ▲ ▲ ▲ ▲ ▲ ▲ ▲ ▲ ▲ ▲ ▲ ▲

N THE FALL OF 1972 some Cherokees from Oklahoma retraced their own tribe's "Trail of Tears" and then joined up with representatives from other Indian nations that had been winding their way eastward in a caravan, the "Trail of Broken Treaties." They had stopped at reservations along the way, gathering strength; by the time they reached Wounded Knee in South Dakota their line of cars and trucks was seven miles long. An observer said, "That's one hell of a war party."

But when they reached Washington, D.C., they said their protest would be entirely peaceful and dignified. They planned to invite senators to a meal of corn soup and fry bread, then discuss a twenty-point proposal on how to improve U.S.-Indian relations. Official Washington, however, gave them a big brush-off; one Indian leader said, "What do we have to do to get some attention—scalp somebody?" The longer the Indians were ignored, the more colorful their rhetoric became. A speaker on the steps of the BIA office on Constitution Avenue shouted into the microphone, "You have taken our sacred Black Hills, the dwelling place of our spirits, and you have defiled it with Mount Rushmore. Those four gleaming white faces look down as if to say, 'We are your conquerors.' Keep it well guarded. We intend to obliterate it."

In early November, just before election day, they decided to stage a sit-in. Not, they insisted, an occupation. They had a parade of celebrity supporters—from the left, Stokely Carmichael, and from the right a weird fundamentalist minister, the Reverend McIntyre (who never did seem to figure out who was who or what was going on). Then the Indians stormed the BIA building and locked themselves in. A D.C. riot squad tried to clean them out that evening; it was an ugly scene, the police beat the hell out of them. Teenagers started to tear things apart, and the conservative tribal chairmen couldn't hold them. Some of the kids put up a fight with bows and arrows. One of them happily showed the TV cameras how to tape a scissors to a busted-off chair leg and make yourself a tomahawk. Some of the young men were putting on war paint. For five days it was a Buffalo Bill Wild West show.

When the demonstrators finally walked out of the building, on November 9, they left considerable damage behind them. They had stolen documents that demonstrated "decades of bad faith of the white man." The secretary of the interior said, "It is a shame that a small, willful band of malcontents should try to wreck the headquarters of the government's chief instrument for serving the Indian community." A spokesman for the protesters said that there was now extensive damage in rooms where they had done no damage at all. Walls were printed with slogans and names where there had been nothing at departure time. The paint, the spokesman said, appeared fresh, evidence of the old trick of slipping feds in as agents provocateurs.

Mescalero's little moment in the national spotlight was provided by Barnabas Lester. He was in Washington on quite another matter, testifying before a congressional committee regarding oil and gas leases on Apache land. And he was reported to have said, "I admire the feathers on the demonstrators' heads—but I worry about the feathers *in* their heads." He said the time had come for the Indian people to realize that they had to give up running around in warbonnets and begin appearing in court wearing three-piece suits. On the national networks, he issued a warning from the steps of the Capitol: "If any of these thugs show up on my reservation, I will personally cut his braids off."

There was much moaning and groaning in Mescalero. Silas was especially disturbed about the "feathers in their heads" remark—Silas could not believe his grandfather had actually said that. Annie had long ago worked out the metaphor: her father-in-law was Thieu or Ky in Vietnam, a petty dictator propped up by the United States; what we had here was a tiny band of guerrilla warriors challenging the most powerful nation in the world; Barnabas Lester's reservation was a corrupt native government, repressing its own people, and doing it for a big foreign power that was willing to pay him handsomely.

When Barnabas got back to Albuquerque, he was interviewed at the airport; he said these were very dark times for the American Indian, and he had the authority to hire a private police force to secure peace on his reservation. He said that AIM (the American Indian Movement) had its roots in cities, where there was ugliness and violence and brutality; the AIM people had lost touch with their native traditions and had forgotten what life was like back behind the "buckskin curtain."

In that atmosphere, plenty hot to begin with, something truly stupid and terrible happened. Rufus, my ambulance driver, poor old Rufus Sundayman, got himself all liquored up and made a royal pain of himself at an American Legion dance in Ruidoso. Half a dozen legionnaires kicked the shit out of him, just for the fun of it, stripped him naked from the waist down and paraded him in front of the hooting crowd at the dance. Rufus was thrown out into the street; some legionnaires dumped him in front of a laundromat. Rufus made it back to the reservation, back to his shack where he kept those savage dogs. We knew from a little story in the local newspaper that an Indian had been mistreated this way, but we didn't know it was Rufus Sundayman until his body was discovered three days later. Apparently his dogs had eaten some of him.

Then all hell busted loose. Our community was still a bit raw and nervous from the Christina Clark case, the violent powwow in D.C., and Barnabas's flamboyant response. Now the shaming and beating and death of Rufus Sundayman led some demonstrators returning from Washington, D.C., to visit Mescalero, New Mexico. Gradually the town began to fill up with little bands from all over. I couldn't identify them, but Silas jumped into the thick of it, and he was out every night. Breathlessly he told me we had Papagos and Pimas from Arizona, White Mountain Apaches, the Cherokees from Oklahoma, Navajos, Pueblos, Arapahos, we even had Agua Calientes from California. At the funeral for Rufus Sundayman, the little Dutch Reformed church was surrounded by Indians beating a mournful dirge on their drums and chanting lamentations to the iron sky.

At 1:00 A.M. the phone rang, and Annie answered it. I didn't hear her say much after the initial hello, but something loud about her silence woke me up. Then she said, "Yes, he'll be there, soon as he can," and hung up the phone. She lay back down, muttered one of her little "ouches" that came so frequently now whenever she moved, however carefully.

I said, "What is it?"

She took a minute. Then: "There's been a fight. Two men badly hurt." I thought she was finished, but after another silence, lasting some time, she said, "It's Leonard. Silas's father. He's been shot."

I stared at the darkness. "Did you know he'd come back?"

"Oh, Leonard comes back—every once in a while."

Which, I realized as I was stumbling into my clothes, did not exactly answer my question. I leaned down and kissed her on the cheek. She reached up, touched my face, and said, "You're supposed to take the ambulance."

I still wasn't fully awake when I went out the front door wondering if Rufus would be sober. Then I shook my head and whispered to myself, "No, Rufus isn't sober, Rufus is dead." I rousted out the other driver, Woodrow Wilson, and in a few minutes we were on our way to an outlying little town on the northeastern corner of the reservation. When we arrived we drove through a bunch of small shacks; usually they had three rooms, a living room with a kitchenette in it, a bathroom, and a bedroom. They were often occupied by families with five or six children. A number of Indians milled around just outside one of the little shacks, and later I pieced the story together. Julio Martinez (half Indian, half Mexican) had come home pretty well lit up, and he found his wife, Doris, doing it big time with Leonard Lester. Doris was now standing around crying in her pink bathrobe; I figured she was in her late teens or early twenties, a Mexican girl, quite pretty, with a lovely little figure. I already knew from Annie that Leonard was a bad actor, though strikingly good-looking and I guess rather charming. Apparently he and Doris were really going at it when Julio burst in on them. Leonard jumped out of bed, grabbed his pants, pulled out a hunting knife, and leaped at Julio as he came across the room. Leonard got in one good strike, slicing Julio's face from the middle of his forehead all the way down to his jaw, a deep sweeping gash that didn't really penetrate anything but caused a copious flow of blood. Julio jumped back at Leonard, knocked the knife aside, got him down on the floor, and started beating on his head. Leonard was not moving. Julio ran out to his truck, got his shotgun, and ran back to the house, where Leonard had got up again and had put his pants on. Julio came through the door and blasted Leonard from a distance of about four feet—Julio had aimed to make sure Leonard wasn't going to bother anybody's wife anymore, but he missed the mark and got him through the top of the leg rather than directly in the groin. Leonard collapsed. That was the situation when Woody and I arrived in the ambulance.

The state policeman, who had gotten there ahead of us—the one who had radioed back to the tribal police chief—had had the good sense to put some pressure on Leonard's leg, which was the only reason he was alive. He looked awful. So did Julio, you could see his skull at the top of the wound, and a flap of skin hung down over the eye. But he wasn't in any mortal danger, so I sent him with the policeman to the hospital in Roswell (where they spent over two hours sewing him up). I turned my attention to Leonard. It is unbelievable what a 12-gauge shotgun will do when fired from four feet. The damage was terrific. The shot had completely missed Leonard's penis and scrotum; it hit just to the right, through the femoral triangle, where all the major nerves and arteries come together, and the veins going to the aorta to supply the leg. It was a huge gaping hole, an injury too high up for anybody to put a tourniquet on, and whoever had put a dirty shirt in there had saved Leonard's life. When we put him in the ambulance he was white as a sheet, but he had a reasonable pulse. We drove him down to Mescalero, and I had the police call ahead so that Max and our emergency-room staff were expecting us.

As usual, Max was superb. We got a couple of liters of saline and a couple of units of blood into Leonard, which brought a little pink back into his cheeks. We took him up to the OR and went to work on the leg. I assisted, partly

because there was nobody else at that hour and partly because I wanted to do my best for Silas's father. But I really
did it because I so enjoyed watching Max work. He amazed
me with his quickness. The first thing we had to do with
Leonard was to get proximal control of the bleeding, the
vein and artery were just blown away. His having put his
pants back on made our work all the more difficult: he had
denim and buckshot driven into the tissues and muscles;
the artery, nerve, and vein had been severely disrupted. Max
immediately made a quick incision in the lower part of the
left abdomen and got arterial clamps on the iliac artery.
Then we went back to the wound to see specifically what
damage had been done; in the thigh, bundles of muscle
were hanging by their remaining threads, barely covering
the underlying femoral artery, which had been ripped in
three places and was clearly not going to be reconstructable.
The largest branches of the femoral vein had been ripped
off by the blast, but they had contracted enough on their
own to control hemorrhage. Max went to the other leg and
scrubbed up the inner side of the right thigh; he removed
a branch of the saphenous vein, the shallow vein that you
can almost see on your own thigh. He took out a four-inch
piece of that vein while I debrided the major wound and
fished out as much buckshot and denim as I could. Max
very neatly took the piece of vein he'd cut out and put a
graft in, tied off the vein there, because you don't really
need that, and we flushed out the wound with liter after
liter of saline. We put multiple drains in and closed it up.

I figured Leonard would walk with a little limp for the
rest of his life, but he did just fine. A real Apache. Neither
man had charges filed against him. Some months later Julio

stole a car, the Tularosa police chased him halfway up Sierra Blanca at high speed, and Julio's car flipped over, coming to an abrupt halt on an embankment cut out of the rock. He was killed instantly. After a short time Doris went back to Mexico.

"BRAVES, YOU ARE LIKE little children; you know not what you are doing when you murder white people. You are full of the white man's devil water. You are like dogs in the Hot Moon when they run mad and snap at their own shadows."

—Little Crow

N▲ ▲ ▲ ▲ ▲ ▲ ▲ ▲ ▲ ▲ ▲ ▲ ▲ ▲ ▲ ▲ ▲ ▲ ▲
O W M E S C A L E R O was crowded with dozens of activists, law-enforcement officers, media people, and curiosity seekers. A rumor ran around that Leonard had been wounded by an AIM gunman while standing guard at his father's house. One also heard that Leonard was a big wheel in AIM and that he'd been shot by one of his father's goons. With that many people, in that flammable situation, gun dealers were doing a land-office business. The lobby of the hospital quickly became a kind of headquarters. In the parking lot a soup kitchen and a sound truck materialized; the air was full of public-service announcements and urgent political speeches.

AIM's formal symbol was an upside-down American

flag, the international distress signal. Nobody could deny that Native Americans were in distress—except for the local John Birch Society, two of whose members came out to denounce AIM as a "Hate Whitey" movement led by Communists who were "*really* red Indians." But some of our local Apaches themselves had no use for the AIM troops, calling them a bunch of malcontents from the red ghettos back east, city Indians, ex-convicts who had been confused by the white man's manners and who had lost touch with the old ways. Woodrow Wilson shook his head and told me the AIM crowd with their headdresses and warrior talk just excited white folks. Barnabas was quoted in the newspapers as fully expecting to answer his doorbell and find Marlon Brando and Jane Fonda sitting on his front porch. Barnabas called AIM "a band of hooligans, juvenile delinquents, and rowdies." Silas told me that this was an old white trick, setting Indians against Indians.

In the hospital I made my rounds, treating the wounded and sick (we had one very bad afternoon when a dozen people came down with food poisoning). I could hear the loudspeakers out in the parking lot, snatches of speeches about "beef and blankets" and "Remember, before it was the Department of the Interior it was the Department of War" and a woman's litany of praise for "the fish-ins" involving water rights back in 1963 at Franks Landing. A picket line featured big poster-print signs, "REMEMBER RUFUS SUNDAYMAN," "JUSTICE NOW," and (my favorite) "WE SHALL OVERRUN."

The young men in AIM didn't have that hangdog reservation look of many of the guys in Mescalero. One speaker shouted, "No to the necktie, yes to the choker! No to the briefcase, yes to the blanket!" He asked for a show of hands:

"Did you, tell the truth now, how many of you celebrated Thanksgiving? It is the most obscene holiday white Americans celebrate. What does the red man have to celebrate? Look at this upside-down flag—every star in it stands for a state that was stolen from Indians!" He was carrying a medicine pouch. Several young Indians sported the revolutionary uniform: a red headband, earrings, a bone neck choker, an elaborately embroidered vest. Most of the time they were playing drums and singing old Indian songs. It was the biggest show ever to hit Mescalero.

But I watched some of the old people exchanging knowing glances with each other. When a "red power" speaker praised a local Indian woman for rejecting the white man's world and seeking the old truths of the medicine man, the old people knew, as I did, that that was not what she had done; her bacterial endocarditis could have been easily cured, but confused and hopeless, she didn't get the medical help she so desperately needed and it spun out of control. Her useless, meaningless death was turned into the lesson "Be proud." And when a Sioux woman gave an impassioned plea not to get involved in the white man's genocidal birth-control devices—"Do not let them kill the warriors of tomorrow"—I had a stupid little argument with Silas, and I felt so pompously irrelevant I couldn't stand myself. I think it was those goddamn *drums*, hour after hour. Our little hospital was ready to burst at the seams.

One night in the second week, after a heavy snowfall, I sat in Annie's living room listening to Silas, pumped up by it all, grinning. He wasn't stoned, wasn't drunk, just exuberant. Annie had had one of her worst days, even the large doses of codeine weren't working. And Silas hardly seemed to notice, so distracted was he by the circus atmosphere. After I helped Annie to bed, Silas said to me, "AIM is doing for us what the Panthers are doing for black people, what the Weathermen are doing for young white people."

"*Exactly!*"

He looked at me, puzzled. Then he scowled. "Mom's right, you're conservative."

I didn't say anything.

"Well," he went on, "it's like the old days—except now, instead of being 'hostiles,' we're 'militants.'" Silas clapped his hands together three times. "Indians have been programmed to accept defeat. Now we are getting our heads de-fucking-programmed!" He went on about how he was going to get himself an eagle feather for "dusting a pig."

I said, "No, you're not."

He looked at me.

"No, you're not," I said again, and left the room. I brooded in the kitchen.

I heard his mother call him. And when I heard her bedroom door close, and when another five minutes went by, I realized, suddenly, what was going on. Annie had made it clear to me that she wanted to be the one to tell Max Rubenstein about her cancer. And she had done that. Max and I had talked, slowly, quietly, making sure that we had missed nothing, making sure that we were doing all that could be done. Max had talked long-distance with old friends of his and with former professors at Ann Arbor. I had talked for an hour with a guy I knew at Einstein in Philadelphia. But Annie had been unable to tell Silas. She kept putting it off.

Now, as I stood in the kitchen, late at night, somehow I knew Annie was telling her son that she was going to die. I took a deep breath. I must have held that breath for an hour—certainly I did metaphorically. And at last, when Silas came back out, he said to me, quietly, intensely, "How long is Mom going to live?"

The cancer, I told him, was moving more rapidly than I had expected. "She has what we call a lytic lesion in the pelvis. From the bone scan we can see other lytic lesions in her backbone. And her legs. And—I'm so sorry, Silas—in her skull. The tumor's metastasizing everywhere. She'll live to see the New Year, maybe even the spring." I put my hand on his shoulder.

He looked at me. "Is this why my dad came back?"

That took me by surprise. I wondered if it were so. I had been distracted at the hospital every day, and I hadn't been able to think things through.

I got the courage to look at him again, and Silas was staring blankly at the stove. He said, "I don't believe this is happening."

I embraced him. We held on to each other.

When I went into Annie's bedroom I thought she was asleep. But as I got quietly, stealthily into bed beside her, she whispered, "Why my father waited to tell me—" She coughed a little, then said to the dark, "Now I understand."

I lay there waiting, but she didn't speak again. She was awake, though, struggling with it for a long, long time.

T▲ ▲ ▲ ▲ ▲ ▲ ▲ ▲ ▲ ▲ ▲ ▲ ▲ ▲ ▲ ▲ ▲ ▲
HE STAFF HAD SPENT a good deal of time decorating the hospital for the Christmas holidays— wreaths, red and green streamers and silver bells, a big tree in the waiting room and a piñata in the children's ward, a cactus with blue and pink winking lights at the nurses' station. But there was no peace on earth for Mescalero that Christmas; the loudspeakers in the parking lot blasted away at the "bobtails" and kept up a fairly steady stream of harangues about "ten thousand American Indian soldiers died in World War I!" and "Never forget the bullshit of 1924 when Indian citizens were given the same rights as other Americans—yeah, *sure!*"

We had had two rather heavy snowfalls by now, and

the temperature hovered below freezing (I treated half a dozen demonstrators for exposure and frostbite). I couldn't tell what the AIM people were really trying to accomplish, since most of their rational economic demands had already been co-opted by Barnabas Lester. The AIMers called him "Uncle Tomahawk," of course, and "the redskin LBJ." The truth was, however, that he had been fighting their battles in courtrooms for two decades.

The demand for "JUSTICE FOR RUFUS SUNDAYMAN" was carried on at the courthouse in Ruidoso. Silas told me that "a fire of suspicious origin" was ignited in the courtroom basement and not a single Indian appeared to help the Ruidoso fire department; when another mysterious fire exploded in the Mescalero sawmill, every fireman was an Apache. The newspapers and the local TV station were having a field day, and one local white rancher distinguished himself on our television screens by saying he wouldn't mind getting out his shotgun and "bagging myself one of them aborigines."

At our little bridge table in front of the fireplace, Max and Annie and Silas and I were discussing it, and Annie said, "You hate most those whom you have injured most." It was a typical Annie pronouncement—a little lecture disguised as a remark. But as I turned to look at her big empty eyes, I just thought it was true. You do "hate most those whom you have injured most." And I loved the woman who talked that way.

She was both a little slow and very determined. The marijuana intensified her air of distraction; Annie was smoking it pretty regularly because it seemed to be about the only thing to ease the pain (whoever says cancer patients aren't helped by pot is crazy). I was holding in reserve the next step, morphine, and I dreaded the day when even that would not do it for her.

She said, slowly, "I went out for half an hour today. I visited the animal graveyard."

Max said, "To see Shep?"

She looked up and smiled, cocked her head a little to one side.

"And Dudley?" Max said. "And Muffin?"

She sighed.

I was shuffling the cards. I stopped and looked at her.

She said, "Then I went down to the pond. I was standing there, leaning on my cane like an old lady, when a big beaver must have seen my shadow on the ice. He led me away from his lodge in the reeds. I stumped along the shore, and we went for a long, long way." She stopped herself and looked at all three of us looking at her, and then she said mournfully, "You men were all out in the world, and I was sad because I had no one to whom I could say, 'Oh, come look!'"

We played one more rubber, Annie had had enough by then, and we just chatted awhile, slowly letting go.

Later on, in the night, in the deep quiet of the dark, we made love. Now it was crazy longing—I was trying to reach my loved one way over there on the other side of unbearable pain. You hear stories about people dying of cancer who, way at the end, want to make love with their partner one last time, no matter how great the pain. It was like that, I guess. You'd think that as a doctor I would know the meaning of pain. But I didn't. I had never seen anybody suffer the way Annie did. All my efforts to relieve that suffering were ineffective. Cancer lived up to its symbol, the crab, chewing at her bones, one by one. She was gradually withering away. Her breasts lost their firmness, her beautiful ass became bony, her menstruation stopped. But when we made love I could feel all the life in her rushing toward me, her sweet frantic whimpers in my ear. I was as careful as I knew how to be. It hurt her, but she wanted to do it. Afterward I would hold her and rock her and sing little lullabies. She would fall asleep, sometimes for three or four hours, before the pain woke her again. One morning after I had been tiptoeing about in the kitchen I came back into our room—she was so still, I thought for a moment I had lost her. Then she opened her eyes, looked at me, and smiled. She started to speak and then drifted back into sleep.

"I WILL NEVER MAKE peace with the Americans. This is the land of our fathers, the land where their bones are buried and whose graves we should defend to our last breaths. This is what I intend to do."

—Tecumseh

A

▲ ▲ ▲ ▲ ▲ ▲ ▲ ▲ ▲ ▲ ▲ ▲ ▲ ▲ ▲ ▲ ▲ ▲ ▲

T 7:00 A.M. ON THE fourteenth of December, Max and I came to work and the bastards wouldn't let us into the hospital. AIM guys with rifles were stationed at all the doors. I had been wondering how long all those people could stand it, in the bitter cold, and now they had decided to occupy the biggest building in town, the building with a clear view down into the valley. Max blew up and screamed at the guards, "You stupid assholes, this isn't a student union, it's a goddamn *hospital!*"

A tough-looking Indian in his mid-twenties seemed to be the guy in charge. He let the two of us in, and we stood arguing with him in the reception area. Three or four nurses were huddled in the hall, scared as hell, watching us. Behind them, like their overseer, stood another AIM guy with a pistol on his hip.

The main man, Thomas Brave Bear, was clearly intelligent, and he chose his words with care. At dawn there had been a little "firefight," and each side said the other side had started it as a provocation. He said a couple of FBI guys had appeared on the scene the night before, and they had been arming "Lester's goons." Max was only half listening, pacing back and forth; Thomas Brave Bear talked softly and directly to me. He said, "A lot of weapons got distributed. Nobody really knows where they're all goin'." He even smiled a little, almost shyly, when he said to me, "The forces of law and order are mainly getting in each other's way. It is so fucking stupid."

Max vehemently broke in. "We have old people here who can't walk. Newborn babies. Wounded people that can't be moved. Go have your revolution somewhere else. Are you out of your minds?"

Facing that, Thomas Brave Bear's eyes went suddenly into self-doubt.

I said to him, "We take care of wounded on both sides. Any side. We have to do that."

Thomas Brave Bear faltered again. "We want this over as soon as possible. It all depends on Lester's next move."

Max said, "You got a gun to his head, what the *hell* do you think you are doing?"

I realized how scared I was when the thought passed through my mind that I didn't want Max hurt. I wanted him for future usefulness, I couldn't do this all by myself. I knew I had just given up the fight in the first round. Now I was just figuring out how to manage the least harm. And I needed him. I said, "Max, can it."

His green eyes were jumping around all over the place. " '*Can* it'?"

I looked away. And then I grabbed him, I caught hold of his left arm just above the elbow. "Let's go to work."

As we went to our offices, I was thinking to myself, "We're not doctors, we're medics, God help us."

"My son, no one will help you in this world. Run to that mountain and come back. Be strong. My son, no one is your friend. Your legs are your friends. Your brain is your friend. Your eyesight is your friend. Your hands are your friends. Some day you will be with people who are starving, and you will have to get something for them. If you go somewhere you must beat the enemy who is attacking you before he gets over the hill. You must get in front of him and bring him back dead. Then you will be the only man."

—Apache father

▲ ▲ ▲ ▲ ▲ ▲ ▲ ▲ ▲ ▲ ▲ ▲ ▲ ▲ ▲ ▲ ▲ ▲ ▲ ▲

N THE MIDDLE OF ALL that desperate con-
fusion and violence, I stopped by to see a patient at home,
Mary Brazil, an old woman who had been an elementary-
school teacher here for many years. Her biggest concern
was that she would put people to inconvenience by dying.
When I had first met her, last summer, she was losing
weight, suffering indigestion and diarrhea; she had several
symptoms that suggested malabsorption, something wrong
with the lining of the intestine or something amiss with her
pancreatic secretions. Patients with it just don't absorb their
food very well. I sent her down to El Paso, and they took
a small-bowel biopsy. She swallowed a little capsule hooked
to a thin tube; when an X ray shows it to be in the right

place, you just suck on the tube with a syringe, and a piece
of bowel is sucked into the capsule and then sheared off by
a little guillotinelike blade. The lining of her intestine was
full of white blood cells—but unusual white blood cells
called eosinophils, often associated with allergy. Eosino-
philic gastroenteritis is a rare disorder, but easy to diagnose
and easy to treat, with cortisone. In a couple of weeks Mary
was a new woman. Her strength returned, and she experienced weight gain and cessation of discomfort. In late fall
she began to have the same kind of trouble, and I put her
on medication; within a week everything was back to normal, and she told me I was a miracle man.

But in early December she began to dwindle, feeling
bad all over, tired and weak, and her legs were swelling
up. I thought it was a recurrence of our old problem, but
this time when I got a blood count she was quite anemic
and she had a platelet count of 4 million, instead of the
normal 240 million. In a case such as this, a patient usually
gets a fatal hemorrhage from someplace or other, often in
the brain. I was pretty sure she had an acute leukemia. I
admitted her to the hospital, we did a bone marrow, and
it confirmed what I expected. It is a lethal disease for a
person her age. I gave her some blood, gave her some
platelets, and she instantly felt much better. We sat down
and had a long discussion about whether she should take
chemotherapy. At best it might offer a 50 percent chance
of remission, from six months to a year, before she started
going down the tubes. I can talk a patient into taking
chemotherapy when I really feel it is the thing to do, and
in this case I did, because Mary Brazil enjoyed life so much
that if given a few months relatively symptom free it would
be nice for her. She thought long and hard about it for

several days. And then she said no. That's not the way she
wanted to do it. She was going to go home and die. She
didn't want to cause anybody any real difficulty. Knowing
that I can do something, and then having someone tell me
they don't want it done, is a little hard to swallow. But I
could see her point. So I made arrangements for Loretta,
our public health nurse, to come in and help.

Within two weeks Mary began to fade very rapidly.
Platelets only last about a week, and she didn't have any
bone marrow to make new ones, they were all being re-
placed by malignant cells. That night when I went to see
her at home she was alert but quite tired. She couldn't
move. But she was not in pain. I sat down and talked with
her about dying. She wanted to do it with dignity. And,
by God, that's what she was doing. I think I felt no different
from how a close relative would have felt. I had no reason
to examine her or to do any of the things doctors do. So
we just talked. We decided she wouldn't have any more
visitors. I might come again, though we both knew that
she might not make it through the weekend. This might
be the last time we would see each other. After a while she
asked me if I had a needle that would make it all go away
very peacefully so that nobody would have to be bothered
about her over the weekend. I sat there beside her. I looked
at her. At her age, and after all her suffering, she seemed
to me extraordinarily beautiful. I said, "Mary, I really love
you. You're a wonderful person. I'm here just as a friend.
And let me tell you something. I am going to miss you."
In a faint little ironic way, she said, "Me, too."

I sat there a little longer and then walked out of the
room. I guess I sort of just lost it. Loretta was there, and
she came up to me and asked, "What should we do now?"

I said, "I'll tell you in a minute." I wandered into a dark corner of the house. After a bit I got my composure back, and I told Loretta that our only concern was to keep our patient comfortable. Mary Brazil lay there with a day or two of life left in her; she knew only vaguely, if she knew at all, what was going on in her Mescalero. She just told me that there is nothing nicer than life, and, Jim, you'd better enjoy yours, she had enjoyed hers. Sunday night she died.

▲ ▲

C O U L D N ' T   K E E P   T R A C K of whose side I was on. There was the extremely painful and subtle war of Indian versus Indian, and there was the obvious war between red man and white man. I was patching up victims whoever they were, in the ER and on the operating table, so I never knew quite what the score was—the sides kept changing and eliding and tearing apart. Some of "the goons" had first gone to AIM, then found out that AIM didn't have any money. So they went to Barnabas Lester. They were hired guns. Meanwhile, a new litany of protest was blaring out of the loudspeakers in the hospital's parking lot: "Burn down Saint Joseph's! It's the white man's religion. Run that priest off our land." I was told that our

Catholic church had closed its doors to AIM; apparently the presiding priest, Father Michael, feared that his church's financial support would be jeopardized.

Although I was all for getting the antagonists out of my hospital, the new anti-Catholic tirades were alarming enough to send me across the valley to Saint Joseph's Mission, the only other big structure on the reservation. Saint Joseph's had taken over twenty years to build. It stood, a powerful stone edifice, on a little butte; to walk into its cavernous sanctuary was like a brief walk into Gothic Europe. I lit a candle for Annie, and I sat for a while in a front pew, staring at a wonderful painting of the "Apache Christ," the sunlight streaming down over it. Then I spoke with Father Michael, a Franciscan; he looked like some Hollywood idea of Jesus, dark beard and brilliant blue eyes. A very strange man. He asked me, "Do you still admit a patient with a bad headache and take off his leg?" He seemed to have shuttered himself up in his holy place; he had very little sense of the drama playing itself out in our community. No, Father Mike was all wrapped up in a play he was writing about Our Lady of Guadalupe. He was having a tough time with the miracles. After a while I realized why. So deep was his faith that he never questioned the literal truth of the saintly lady appearing in midair, and he was afraid it would look "fake" on the stage.

We had the damnedest conversation. On the way back to the hospital, I asked myself why I had taken the time and trouble to meddle with priestcraft. But when I went through the little gauntlet of AIM guys at the hospital door, I found Annie in her nurse's uniform. I took her into my office. "Oh, sweetheart, you are in no condition to—"

"Let me be of help." Her face drawn, her big eyes bright

with pain and medication. "Let me, Jim. Please let me *do* something."

I went against my best judgment and let her work with a burn victim. She could wrap the wounds in antibiotic-coated gauze and change the dressings. The guy had third-degree burns on 40 percent of his body and would most probably die. If he didn't, I was ready to send him to El Paso or Roswell for skin grafting.

People were brought in from little skirmishes, ugly little outbursts here and there. Both sides were trigger-happy. I spent long hours removing necrotic tissue destroyed by the bullets. One young AIM warrior had a gut wound; I was sure that either his colon or the small bowel had been penetrated in one of several places. I had to go in and wash out the abdomen with liters of saline and repair each hole one by one. He had a really dirty colon wound, with fecal contamination of the abdominal cavity. I called on Max, who brought out the proximal colon and performed a nifty little colostomy, which would work until everything simmered down. Another kid had taken a shot in the pancreas, and Max threw up his hands in despair. He put drains in, to get rid of infection, but he knew that he would have to go back two or three times to drain abscesses. I performed my very first splenectomy (it's virtually impossible to repair a gunshot wound in the spleen). Annie assisted; she came in scrubbed up as a surgical nurse and was actually quite helpful, though her presence was extremely distracting to me. Whenever she had to walk a distance of over six or seven feet, she used a cane; I believed she was now experiencing her first pathological fractures. She hobbled in and out of rooms like a ghost.

In the ER I was administering to a U.S. marshal who

had been nicked in his left arm. He was a tough, likable guy. Annie had been giving him a little lecture on politics when he suddenly turned on her. "All we are trying to do, goddamn it, is to stop you fucking Indians out here from killing each other."

"Hold still," she said.

"Yeah? Look, lady, you hold your tongue, and I'll hold still. What the fuck do you mean this is 'political'? It's about fucking *booze*. Pardon my French. I'm not out to get these AIM guys. If AIM gives you Indians pride, then I'm all for it. But what are they shooting at *me* for? I never hurt an Indian in my life."

The two of them kept at it all through the procedure. I had no idea why their exchanges struck me as funny, but I found myself smiling a little.

Along toward evening a tear-gas canister came rolling in the front door. The windows in the lobby hadn't been opened in thirty years, so I took a chair and smashed one open. I thought we were in big trouble, now the whole thing was going to blow. My instinct was confirmed when Annie grabbed hold of me in the hallway and said she had just talked with Silas, something catastrophic was going on down in the valley. "Jim," she said, "*go*. We've got to *stop* it!"

Remembering my experience with Father Michael, I went flying down the hill on another wild-goose chase. I could see ahead of me two helicopters sweeping over the snowy trees. And when I arrived in front of the general store my heart stopped: parked in a long line, a dozen yellow school buses. I could hardly believe my own eyes—out of the buses came at least a hundred men, the biggest men I'd ever seen, they all looked like NFL linemen. Dressed in riot gear, they had helmets, bullet-proof vests, automatic weapons, rocket launchers, hand grenades, M-16s. In the gathering darkness, I walked around quietly and tried to look as if I knew what I was doing; I found out that these men were going to spend the night on cots set up in the gymnasium. Next morning they were going to make a frontal assault on the hospital. Splashing about in the muddy snow, they looked invincible.

For some weird reason, as I fled back up the hill, I remembered a Boy Scout jamboree when I was just a kid, the night we played capture-the-flag. Somehow I had got behind the enemy's line in a little area of high grass, and I stayed there, hushed, for over an hour. Enemy scouts would pass by so close that I could touch them. It was tremendous fun lying there in the damp grass, I almost laughed out loud. Now, in Mescalero, I remembered that delirious sensation of concealment as I made my way up to Barnabas Lester's big white house. To the armed guard on his front porch, I said, "I have to talk to the boss."

"Until i was about ten years old I did not know that people died except by violence. That is because I am an Apache."

—James Kaywaykla

B ▲ ▲ ▲ ▲ ▲ ▲ ▲ ▲ ▲ ▲ ▲ ▲ ▲ ▲ ▲ ▲ ▲ ▲ ▲

A R N A B A S   W A S   C L E A R L Y   worn out, sitting in his old green chair and issuing orders by telephone. About the room were strewn little plates of half-eaten sandwiches and empty coffee cups. It was almost dark, just one low lamp gave off an amber glow. When Barnabas finished on the phone he looked up. "Well, doctor, how can you help me?"

I told him what I had just seen.

"So," he said, "they're here."

"They sure as hell are."

He vaguely motioned for me to sit on the couch, which I did. He yawned and took off his glasses.

I said that I was not hysterical. I said I was not an alarmist.

He said, "Glad to hear it."

I told him what it had been like in the hospital for the past days. The young AIM men in there were prepared to die for their people. I had not the slightest doubt that they would not be taken out of there alive. I pleaded for time. "You have all the chips. You know you can work this thing any way you want to. Please save lives."

He just looked at me with those cold, black Apache eyes.

I said, "The streets will run red with Indian blood."

"I thought you said you weren't an alarmist."

"I'm not. But if you let things go on the way they're going now, at least a dozen people will be dead by noon tomorrow."

Barnabas started to say something. Thought better of it. He knew I was just an outsider. He sat there. He did not want to listen to me. And then he walked out his front door. He was conferring with that big guard. Barnabas came back in, sat down in the green chair again, and picked up the phone. He waited, still thinking, and then dialed.

I suspect something had been worked out earlier. A prior deal had been done. The conversation that followed, I swear it sounded like two old buddies planning a fishing trip. On this end, Barnabas even laughed a couple of times. But it was the single most valuable thing I saw anybody do during that awful time. Barnabas said into the phone, "Well, I'll tell you, Fred, I think your men will enjoy a far better night's sleep in their own homes."

They talked on for a few more minutes, during which

Barnabas lied, he said the tribal police were on top of things. I stepped out onto the front porch and looked out over the lights in the valley, all the trees and the land covered with snow.

It was as pretty as a Christmas card.

When I came back in, we didn't speak for a while. Then, out of nowhere, he said, "Frankly, son, I just work here."

Shit, I was ready to kiss his ring, Don Barnabas. I wasn't sure whether I'd saved his life or just made it a lot harder.

As if to help me, he said, "When you get to be my age, son, you'll find that you shouldn't take yourself too seriously."

"Even if you're a chief?"

"Oh." He smiled. "Especially if you're a chief."

Our greatest danger was safely behind us, but we still weren't out of the woods. Random sniper fire resulted in a steady flow of casualties in the ER, along with our usual crowd of drunks who had hurt themselves, victims of car wrecks, various random illnesses and accidents. I was surviving on very little sleep, catnaps in my office, and I noticed my temper running short. I was shouting at people. Passing by an elderly Indian woman who was praying out in the parking lot, I heard a trooper ask her, "You trying to make it rain?" At once furious, I remembered Annie telling me about Kit Carson's soldiers, the "long knives," who liked to play catch with the severed breasts of Indian maidens. So I walked up to this U.S. marshal and said to him, "You're one big brave man. Making fun of an old woman. Shame on you. Shame on you." He looked at me as if I were really losing it. And maybe I was.

I went into the hospital and made it through the crowded hallways to find Annie sitting in my office. She looked a little better, I thought, her eyes alert. But she was trembling a little, and after I had closed the door she whispered, "Leonard's the snitch."

"Excuse me?"

"It's Leonard. I know it, I heard his voice on the walkie-talkie."

I searched her eyes. "On the walkie-talkie?"

"It's what we thought in the first place."

Not having had a clear thought in the first or any other place, I couldn't follow. The only recent rumor I'd heard was that Lester had come back because he'd done something that got him expelled from the police force in Texas.

Annie had her conspiracy face on, that expression I used to kid her about. But I was glad to see some of the old vitality.

"He's what they call a 'loaned agent.'"

"Loaned?"

"Yes. His expulsion from the police force was rigged. All rigged. They did it to give him credibility when he talked to the AIM people."

I asked her to take it slow, but she rambled on about how much Leonard had stolen from the AIM war chest, at least fifty thousand dollars from wealthy left-wing supporters.

"Sweetheart, you heard all this on a walkie-talkie?"

"No, of course not. Don't do that, Jim. What I heard on the walkie-talkie—well—" She sat silent awhile, shivering. She whispered, "Poor Silas. It'll hurt him. Oh, Jim, I don't want Silas to know."

"Honey, what can I do?"

"They're planning an attack on the hospital."

"No, they're not. I told you, Barnabas put a stop to it. All those national guardsmen are gone."

"The marshals aren't gone."

"Well, they're not going to storm the hospital."

"I don't know, Jim. I don't know."

"Look, sweetheart, I'll talk to Leonard. I'll pretend I'm just looking in on him, checking his progress."

"Be careful. You don't know what he—oh, Jimmy, you don't know."

When I did check in on Leonard, he was sitting up in bed, his eyes closed. Jesus, he was a good-looking bastard. He became aware of my presence and opened his eyes. He said slowly, "I hear you saved my life."

"Don't thank me. Thank the other guy."

"The fairy?"

I looked at him. "The man who saved your life isn't a fairy."

"Seemed like he was."

I examined the thigh wound. My bedside manner, I'm afraid, was not the best. But Leonard didn't say a word, didn't even let out a whimper. Everything seemed to be in order, and as I was starting to turn away Leonard stopped me. "Doc, Annie doesn't look so good."

I waited.

"What's the matter with her? Looks like you dicking her doesn't exactly agree with her."

I didn't want to kill Leonard Lester. I didn't even want

Leonard Lester dead. I wanted Leonard Lester never to have existed at all. But what I did, after I got hold of myself, was tell him the truth.

He was very surprised. He said, "I'm real sorry to hear that."

The emotion seemed genuine enough, and while I had him off guard I asked, "You working for AIM or for your father?"

The sorrow did not entirely leave his face. All he did was look at me with it.

Later that day, in my office, I told Annie that I hadn't been able to discover whether or not Leonard was a "loaned agent" (and I never did figure it out). I also told her about the sadness in his eyes when I told him about her.

She looked away, as if she didn't want me to see the expression on her face. She didn't say anything for a while. And then she muttered, "Before Leonard went to Vietnam, he told me—oh, Jimmy, I don't know—he told me that he was an *Apache*, and he'd never die in bed." Then she looked at me. She said, evenly, "Neither will I."

We were joined by an old-time Apache medicine man, and he saw a few older people. His anesthesia was the redwood herb, his surgical thread was deer sinew, and he used gopher dust to stop any bleeding. His success rate was about the same as ours.

One of the saddest, stupidest things I saw (I still dream about it) was an old horse, shaggy with winter, a big brown horse with a black mane and tail. Through a window at the end of the corridor, I looked out and I saw the horse shot down. It got up, and somebody shot it down again. Up, and shot down. Blood was pouring out of the horse's side, and finally it didn't get up anymore. I couldn't make sense of that pointless cruelty. Target practice? And then, on my way to the bullpen, I faltered a little when I remembered Thomas Brave Bear shouting through the microphone, "They can't starve us out of here—we'll eat horse, and dog, and cat, and mice—" That poor old horse was food?

On the last night that the hospital was under siege, I had been busy delivering a baby. When we finished—a remarkably easy delivery, all I had to do was catch—I heard gunfire out in the parking lot. We had become pretty used to the sound of gunfire by then, but Woodrow Wilson came running up to me saying the phone lines had been cut. A very odd brilliant white light was coming in from out front, and when I got to the lobby I could see floodlights and also something that looked like tear gas or smoke, a kind of supernatural fog. It was quite beautiful if you just forgot what it was. Then I heard a marshal's deep voice, amplified: "These fucking Apaches are going wild—*we need protection and we need it now!*" And just after that I could see, out in the parking lot, Annie in her nurse's uniform, with a Red Cross patch, waving her cane—she had a towel or a pillow slip tied onto her cane like a flag of truce. It all happened so fast that I still can't distinguish between what I saw and what I only imagined. In that ghostly white light there was a burst of gunfire near the woodpile down at my old bungalow. I saw a man curled up on the snowy pavement, I think he was the guy Annie was trying to get to. There were several shots from at least two different directions;

Annie, caught in the crossfire, tottered and put her hand up. The force of the blast spun her around, it was as if she had been hurled, and she went down real fast.

In a sudden silence, everything still, I thought Annie was trying to move, to get up. But maybe it was just a reflex, a helpless twitching of her body. Then a lot of people were rushing around, and for a moment I was out there next to Max. Tom Brave Bear had hold of a man's body, half lifting, half dragging it. People were running away into the darkness and colliding with people running toward the light. On the bloody pavement one young man was clearly dead, nothing much left of his face. By the time I got into the ER everybody was screaming, shouting, crying. Blood all over my hands and sleeves, I reached Annie on a stretcher. So far as I could tell, she had put up her hand to shield herself from the floodlights, and the bullet had taken off three fingers, which probably slowed it down a little before it continued on its slightly deflected trajectory. Annie's right arm was mostly blown away, almost severed at the elbow, and our biggest initial problem would be to staunch the horrendous flow of blood. I was working on it, worried that I wouldn't be able to save that arm, when I was pulled bodily away from her. I kicked, kicked like a horse, back there at whoever was grabbing me, and I must've got him, because suddenly I was back over my patient again. Then two big hands came across Annie's body, and those two hands clasped both of my hands and held on. I looked up, I don't know why I needed to, I had already recognized the hands, I loved those hands because I'd watched them perform miracles.

Max, splattered with blood, was looking at me. Later I was told that neither one of us spoke. But somehow I heard my unspoken words, I heard them in my head. I said, "We can't let her bleed to death!" I heard my voice in my head say, "Careful, *careful!*" But Max was holding my hands—Max, the resident master of incredible saves—all he did was look at me with a sadness and a certainty I had never before seen on a human face. Then he let go of my hands. And I stepped back. I stood there at the gurney and watched my Annie die.

"LATE ONE AFTERNOON when returning from town we were met by a few women and children who told us that the white man's troops had attacked our camp, killed the warriors on guard, captured all our ponies, secured our arms, destroyed our supplies and killed our women and children. Quickly we separated, concealing ourselves as best we could until nightfall, when we assembled at our appointed place, a thicket by the river. Silently we stole in one by one. Sentinels were placed, and, when all were counted, I found that my aged mother, my young wife, and my three small children were among the slain. There were no lights in camp, so without being noticed I silently turned away and stood by the river. How long I stood there I do not know."

—Geronimo

T WO OTHER INDIANS were killed that night
—one instantly, a twenty-seven-year-old male from a Pima
reservation in Arizona, and one nineteen-year-old Chero-
kee, we lost him just before daybreak. In the immediate
aftermath I wasn't much good at reading newspaper ac-
counts or watching the local TV news. I kept getting things
mixed up and missing the point. A white trooper in uniform
said, straight into the camera, "Our men can't be held
responsible for some woman on drugs who wants to play
Florence Nightingale."

Thomas Brave Bear said the authorities had tried to
wring information out of him by threatening imprison-
ment—"The keys to your cell are in your mouth."

Performing my rounds like a sleepwalker, I just tried not to make a mistake. A phrase kept drumming in my head, courtesy of Thomas Brave Bear, who said he heard one state trooper say to another, "I guess we sent that squaw to the happy hunting ground."

I thought about that quite a bit. Quite a bit.

Silas was understandably obsessed with the question of who fired the fatal shot. At least I had the sense not to tell him what I was thinking: "It won't bring her back." One night I awakened from a terribly vivid dream: Annie was alive and thought she was pregnant; in my dream she put her arms around me, and I was trying to tell her that her periods had stopped because of the cancer, not because she was bearing our child. But I couldn't bring myself to tell her that.

I think—I hope—I was some help to Silas in arranging the funeral. He showed me what he had chosen to be carved on his mother's headstone:

ANNIE MESSENGER BIRD
1936–1972
She Laid Down Her Life
For Her People

I think I said to Silas, " 'Laid down'—is that right? Lay, laid—I don't— How about 'she *gave*'?"

Sometime later that night he walked into the room and said to me that he had decided "gave" was right.

The funeral was December 20 in Saint Joseph's Mission. The sanctuary was packed with people, there were several rows of Annie's Tularosa High School students, past and present. I sat with Max and the hospital staff. Barnabas Lester rolled Leonard down front in a wheelchair.

All through his eulogy Silas spoke of "my mom," not "my mother." Silas had been crying a lot, and his face was bloated, but he seemed okay and composed, telling us about "Mom's formative years." "Mom" had always fought for her people, and that's what she was doing when she died. Silas was—oh, I don't know—Silas was all lighted up by his mom's spirit. He was so proud of her. He said that Annie Messenger Bird had genuinely loved people and comforted them. All her life, Silas said, his mom had hungered for home, and now at last she had got there, she had returned to the bosom of Mother Earth. It was so simple. The whole church hushed. Then Silas picked up his electric guitar, his "Tele," as he called it, his Fender Telecaster, and he sang one of his mom's favorites from the legendary Ghost Dancing days:

> *The whole world is coming,*
> *A nation is coming,*
> *A nation is coming,*
> *The eagle has brought*
> *the message to the tribe,*
> *The father says so,*
> *The father says so,*
>
> *Over the whole earth they are coming,*
> *The buffalo are coming,*
> *The buffalo are coming,*
> *The crow has brought*
> *the message to the tribe,*

The mother says so,
The mother says so,

Messenger Bird,
Messenger Bird—

And then it was over. It was done. Back at the hospital I was still the doctor, but I had an eerie feeling that the patients and staff were taking care of me. Only three Indians had died that night—some people said that it was almost a blessing, given the potential for a much larger tragedy. By Christmas Day the demonstrators and troops had gone home, wherever home was. Everybody went away. As did I, the following summer, when my two-year hitch was completed. For a while I thought about spending the rest of my life there. But I had to leave. At the farewell dinner Barnabas Lester presented me with a handsome blanket.